STRAIN
THE AGORA VIRUS BOOK 3

JACK HUNT

DIRECT RESPONSE PUBLISHING

Also By Jack Hunt

The Renegades
The Renegades 2: Aftermath
The Renegades 3: Fortress
The Renegades 4: Colony
The Renegades 5: United
Mavericks: Hunters Moon
Killing Time
State of Panic
State of Shock
State of Decay
Defiant
Phobia
Anxiety
Strain

Dedication

For my family.

Prologue

When the power grid shut off, Kate Talbot found herself trapped in an elevator. It was just the beginning of a hellish nightmare. At first, she had expected the power to come back on. It always came back on. It had done this several times over the course of the past two days. Lights would flicker. Monitors would go black and then everything would kick back in.

But not this time.

Shrouded by darkness, contained inside a seven by six foot metal coffin, she could hear the sound of her own blood rushing in her ears as panic crept up in her chest. She leaned forward and felt around for the buttons. Her fingers swept over the circles, pushing them all in a state of desperation.

No response.

"Hello?" she yelled. "Can anyone hear me?"

Her voice echoed in the steel chamber.

She took a few deep breaths. "Don't panic. It will come back on." She hated the dark. Her fingers ran over the concave buttons and she tried again, this time taking her time and slowly going one by one.

Once again, nothing happened.

"Shit!"

Kate slumped down against the side. It shifted ever so slightly and she prayed to God that the wires held. The thought of it dropping made her sweat.

Only thirty minutes earlier she had been working away at the CDC with the grand hope of finding a cure to the Agora Virus, a disease that had already killed thousands around the globe, bringing society to its knees.

Hours of work.

Days of toiling over different samples.

And they still hadn't come close to finding a solution.

Eventually, she knew there was no hope when her

coworkers stopped returning to their workstations. At first, it was just one or two who abandoned their post. Then slowly but surely the group thinned out until there was only her and two others. The expressions on their faces as they gazed around the empty lab spoke volumes. They didn't even need to say anything. One by one they removed their white overalls and walked away.

No one stopped them. No one was left to stop them.

The CDC was as quiet as a library. Her heels clacked along the ground as she made her way down to the internal parking. The lot inside was empty barring one other car. Not once in all the years she'd worked there had she seen it like this. It was always packed. Shifts occurred around the clock. Not now.

Kate had returned to her apartment with the goal of packing what little she had, collecting Tom's gun, and then heading north to the island. She didn't want to be alone and yet that's exactly how she felt. Her apartment was a studio that she had been sharing with Tom prior to his death. The very thought of him brought tears to her eyes.

The CDC, along with a large section of the city, had been barricaded. It was one thing to see it on the news, another to see it in person. She hadn't left the CDC since the virus has spiraled out of control.

On the journey to her apartment block, she took in the sight of the fires that raged out of control. Since the barricades had been breached, all sense of order had fallen by the wayside. Order and decency were a thing of the past. Now, it was every man, woman and child for themselves.

The black Infinity swerved and weaved it's way through the chaotic streets. She had to take a different route home, one that was longer because of the riots, looters and desperate who were taking matters into their own hands.

She navigated down back roads and tried to keep her mind occupied by telling herself that it was going to be okay. Once she made it to Clayton she would be safe. She thought about Frank. Though her life with him had been tough, she had got through it by repeating positive words. He said it didn't have any merit, but she swore by it.

Now, as she dealt with the situation before her, she once again reverted back to affirmations. *You can do this. You are strong. You will overcome.*

What should have taken fifteen minutes to get home took closer to forty. At one point, she had to do a huey in the road because a group of locals had taken up control of a section of the city. They had blocked off the streets with multiple cars, covered the tops in barbed wire that had once been used by the government to keep everyone quarantined.

It was a disaster just waiting to happen.

When she arrived at the luxurious high-rise that Tom said they could afford on both of their salaries, she was pleased to find that it was still in one piece. Many of the buildings nearby were ablaze. How? Why? Who knew what might have caused it. She could still hear in the distance sirens wailing. The last wave of police, firemen and ambulances. Those wouldn't last long. If the CDC had given up, eventually, so would emergency services.

Upon entering the lobby, the electrical grid was still working.

Heck, even Jake Roberts, the security guard on duty, was still manning his post.

But that was then, this was now.

Kate was losing her patience.

After ten minutes inside that darkened elevator, her eyes had adjusted. Kate slammed her fist against the side and screamed for someone to hear her, but no one could. At first, she just assumed it was the elevator. A glitch. Nothing more. They would eventually hear her, pull her out and she would breathe a sigh of relief.

I should have taken the stairs. Why didn't you take the stairs? She thought.

She had never taken the stairs in the two years she had been living there. The apartment block was twenty-one stories high. Out of the entire selection of floors they could have been on, Tom had picked one on the highest.

Before the power went out, she was somewhere

between floor seventeen and eighteen. At least that's what she recalled.

"Come on!"

Her anger was getting the better of her. Out of all the places to get stuck.

Another five minutes passed before she remembered her phone. She patted her jacket down, pulled it out, and slid her thumb across the glossy surface. The screen glowed a bright white, providing her with some badly needed light. It was only partially charged. It wouldn't last. She tried to phone but was getting no signal. Rising to her feet, she moved around in the tight confines holding the cellphone up, thinking that eventually she would get a bar.

"C'mon."

No luck.

She gritted her teeth. "You've got to be joking!"

With no Internet connection and no signal, she was shit out of luck. The first thing she attempted was to pry the doors open. As hard as she tried, she couldn't shift it.

She gazed up at the ceiling above. It was metallic and paneled with small pot lights. She shone the light along the edges looking for some sort of release mechanism. There was nothing. Weren't these things meant to have an emergency hatch? Some kind of handle that could be used in the event someone got stuck inside? Nope. Not this. They were all about appearances. Still, she was determined to find it. It had to be there.

However, the first challenge was to try and figure out how to get up high enough that she could attempt to pry one of the panels loose. She didn't have Frank's height. She was only five-foot three. She stretched out and rose up on her toes and was just able to touch the ceiling. There was a handrail on either side. She attempted to climb up using it but it was impossible. So she did the next best thing. She took a few steps back, placed one foot on it and used it to push herself upward. It wasn't perfect, and she fell on her ass several times but each time she launched upward, she managed to hit the elevator-ceiling panel above her. After the fourth attempt it dropped, ever so slightly. From there, she was able to stand up on her toes and start using some leverage to pry it loose. Fortunately she didn't have to, as it slid to one side. It seemed as if it worked using a mechanism that required it to be pressed then slid to one side. She shifted it over and now found herself staring up into a dark void.

Using her phone, she shone the light upward and could see all manner of steel cables soaring upwards.

"Well, here goes nothing." After multiple failed attempts, she finally did it. Exhausted, sweating and more than pissed off, Kate sat with her feet dangling down into where she had once been confined.

She gazed up into the darkness.

"Hello!" she yelled and her voice echoed off the walls of the shaft.

There was no response.

Navigating her way over to the wall, she noticed there wasn't exactly any ladder that went up, just a whole lot of steel overlapping and cables. "Why me," she grumbled as she began the ascent up to the next floor. She wasn't that far from the eighteenth floor. She stuck her phone in her mouth and made sure to have the light pointing upward as she clambered up, praying to God that she didn't slip. One wrong footing and she would plummet to an early death, or at least break her back.

She pushed the horrific thought from her mind.

If getting out of the elevator was hard, it didn't look as though it was going to be any easier prying the doors open on the eighteenth floor.

When she finally made it up, her hands and clothes were covered in grease. Perched on a ledge no wider than half her shoe, she held on to a cable with one hand and began pulling and pushing at the doors. When that didn't work, she started kicking it as hard as she could, hoping she would raise enough noise that someone would hear and come to her aid. She kicked that bastard door for at least five minutes before giving up. Sweating profusely, she cursed under her breath. There was no way in hell she was going to get through there. Between balancing on the edge, holding on, and trying to get her fingers between the doors, it wasn't working.

She had almost resigned to the fact that she would be trapped in there for hours and likely starve to death when she heard a male voice on the other side.

"Mam."

Kate stuck her phone in her back pocket.

"Oh, thank god." She breathed a sigh of relief. "Jake?"

"Mrs. Talbot. I'll get you out. Give me a couple of minutes."

She exhaled hard and waited for what felt like ten before she heard a clunking sound and the doors were pulled wide. Immediately, she noticed the hallway was dark.

"Here, give me your hand."

He helped her in and she thanked him.

"For a moment I thought everyone had left."

"Oh, most folks have. I'm the only idiot who has stuck around."

"Well I appreciate it. Doesn't this place have a backup generator or something?"

"No, they spent all the money on making it look pretty," he said before chuckling. He had a flashlight in his hand and shone it down the hall. "Will you be okay from here? I need to go level by level and make sure there aren't any other issues. We had looters trying to get in earlier this evening."

She had her hands on her knees and was trying to catch a breath when she nodded. "Oh yeah, don't worry about me."

He turned to leave.

"Jake."

"Yeah?"

"Why are you still here?"

"I needed the money. I just assumed they would figure out this virus issue and open up the barricades. My apartment is beyond."

"You know it's been breached, right?"

"Yeah, I saw that."

"And you still didn't leave?"

He shrugged. "Dumb move, right?"

"I don't know. I only just knocked off forty minutes ago."

He leaned against the wall near the stairwell. "Where's Dr. Jenkins?"

Her eyes dropped and she didn't need to say anymore.

"I'm sorry. That's rough."

"Yeah. I was just going to grab a few things and head out."

"And go where?"

"North, to be with my daughter, and my ex. We have an island near Clayton."

"Room for one more?" He muttered, then acted as though he didn't mean it. Yet she could tell it was a serious question.

She frowned and looked at him closely. "Where's your family?"

"Pennsylvania. Though my grandparents are from here. I moved out here with my girlfriend a year ago. That all went to shit and well, I've been stuck here ever since. I've been thinking of moving back, you know, to be close to family and all, but you know how it goes. You get into a routine and…"

"It takes over."

He nodded and grinned. "Exactly." He paused for a second. "Anyway, I should make sure no one else has gotten stuck in the other elevator, or worse."

"Worse?"

He shook his head and disappeared into the stairwell. Kate rested for a few seconds, staring down the long corridor. She took out her phone and used it to light the way ahead before making her way over to the stairwell and heading up to the twenty-first floor. As she entered the stairwell, she heard voices down below and figured that other residents were coming out to find out what was going on.

Why? It seemed pretty obvious.

Since the virus had spread, the World Health Organization had alerted everyone to stay inside until further notice. While some would heed that warning, others wouldn't. Now with the power down, the streets and buildings in the cities would become a haven for the depraved and desperate.

Her thighs screamed in protest as she ascended three flights of steps. As soon as she approached her apartment, she noticed that the door was slightly ajar. Her brow knit together. She had seen the same thing on several of the other apartments throughout the hallway. Was Jake checking the rooms? Had someone broken in? He had mentioned looters. On an ordinary day, security was tight and people had to be buzzed in, but without any power, none of the cameras would have been working and there were multiple ways into the building: through the underground parking, on the south and east sides, and the main entrance. Any one of the residents could have left a door ajar on their way out.

Nervously, she approached the door and pushed it open. It let out the faintest creak, just enough to cause her pulse to pound. Holding out her phone in front of her, she moved it back and forth. Her own shadow danced on the wall as she eased her way inside.

Suddenly she stopped.

The apartment was split into two levels, the upper contained bedrooms and a main bathroom, and the lower offered a living room and kitchen.

"Hello?" she called out.

There was no answer. She tried the light switches out of habit, but they didn't work. Not hearing any movement, she went over to the front door and closed it behind her. No sooner had she taken a few steps back into the apartment, she heard movement above. She turned her head for just a brief moment; a flash, the sudden crack of a gun going off, and Kate hit the floor.

Chapter 1

Gananoque, Canada.

Two months after outbreak.

"Look, it was an honest mistake!" Frank said, backing up slowly with several beads of blood trickling down his cheek. He eyed the semi-automatic rifle on the ground. It was too far away. Where the hell was Sal when he needed him? His eyes scanned the window; the rear exit door was barricaded with thick planks of wood that had been nailed in. He berated himself for going in there. They didn't need alcohol, but after everything they had been through over the past month, he thought it would be a nice way to show his appreciation for the assistance the other survivors had given.

"You're right about that," the grizzly man said, holding a baseball bat in his hand and moving towards him. He had to have been six foot four, and built like an

American football player. His dark hair was swept back into a ponytail and he was wearing a coonskin hat, a plaid shirt and torn, stone washed jeans. What didn't help was the fact that the baseball bat had nails protruding out of the end and he was swinging it around like a maniac. Frank had come within inches of having it embedded in his skull. Fortunately, he moved just in the nick of time. Instead, the nails scraped the side of his forehead, causing it to bleed. It hurt like a bitch, but he considered himself lucky.

Frank put a hand out, trying to calm him down.

"Now listen up, I didn't know there was anyone in here."

"And that gave you the right to break in?" he paused for a second. "Can't you read?"

There was a sign out front that read: ENTER AT YOUR OWN RISK. Okay, maybe it was pretty clear, but Frank just assumed that they were taking a page out of Sal's book to ward people off. Sal had littered the island in warning signs just like that.

Since the incident with Butch Guthrie, and the destruction of Frank's home, he and the other survivors had taken up residence on Grindstone Island. Butcher's remaining relatives, including Bret, opted to move on to Maine, where his uncle lived. It was a majority vote that was made by those already on the island. After everything that had happened, no one trusted them and though Frank knew that Bret was completely different from Butch, he agreed with the others. He spoke with him briefly before he left and though it pained Bret to know that his brothers were dead, he'd said that Butch had it coming. He'd warned him that it wouldn't end well, but he never listened. Whether he was telling the truth or not was immaterial.

Frank raised his hands and took a few steps back; every now and again he would glance behind to make sure he wasn't about to trip over a chair or table.

"Look, my name's Frank. What's your name?"

The guy smirked. "Oh really? Now you want to get acquainted?"

"Well, I—"

Before he could spit the words from his mouth, the guy lunged at Frank, swinging the baseball bat like the mallet of Thor. Frank sidestepped and cracked him in the side of the face. He shook his hand in pain. It was like hitting granite. The guy must have had a steel jaw. Slowly, the stranger turned his face and gave a toothy grin. Frank tried to vault over a table but the lunatic kicked it out from underneath him and he came down hard on the rosewood flooring. Frank let out a groan. *Oh, God where are you, Sal!*

* * *

Sal swallowed the final mouthful of beer and relished every drop. Gabriel and Zach sat on either side of him in leather lazy-boy armchairs staring a blank wide screen TV.

"You want to pass me those nachos," Sal muttered. He was laid back in his seat, feeling cozy and warm.

"I've gotta say, this little venture into Canada is turning out alright," Gabriel said. They had managed to raid an apartment above a cleaned out convenience store.

Zach had found four beers in a fridge that was no longer working. After the power went out, they thought it would be a good time to stock up on items that would perish over the coming days. Clayton had become a ghost town and what little remained in stores was soon looted. Gabriel had made the suggestion of heading across the water to Gananoque and seeing what they could find. After they arrived, they wished they had gone there sooner. They had only been there half an hour when they came across the apartment above the convenience store. It had more in it than the store below. Whoever owned it had left in a hurry, leaving behind several bags of nachos, four beers, three boxes of cereal and nine cans of tuna. After filling up several pillowcases with the goods, they headed down and began exploring the stores on the street. That's when they came across a furniture and electronics store. Beside it was a hardware shop. The windows in the front were already shattered, so gaining access was easy enough. Once inside, Gabriel and Zach went on a spree, smashing up items that would be of no use. Sal knew it was a way to blow off steam; it was the small things that gave them pleasure now. After the power went out, frustration abounded on the island. Even though they had backup power generators that were powered by fuel and by the sun, the power had to be used sparingly. All of which meant at times they had to cook like their ancestors — over a grill using wood or charcoal. Getting rid of human waste wasn't pretty either, even though they had a few composting toilets.

Water was another thing. They had plenty in storage, and there were of course the rivers and streams in the area.

Fortunately, Butch had already stocked up on a shit load of survival gear, like Lifestraw personal water filters and several large water filtration systems. Small things like flashlights, lamps, candles and batteries now became the norm. That's what they were searching for in the town. They couldn't get enough of them. Unfortunately, it looked like others must have had the same idea. The place had been torn apart except for a few items.

The sixty inch flat screen TV they were staring at had a crack in the front, as if someone had taken a hammer to it.

"You think we should save this last beer for Frank?" Zach asked. All of them had been eyeing it since they had polished off their own.

"Yeah, he's probably dying for a drop of alcohol," Gabriel muttered.

* * *

Frank tossed the bottle of bourbon at the man. He ducked and it shattered against the wall.

"That was an expensive bottle."

"Well, maybe if you calm down a minute we can have a drink."

The burly man vaulted over the bar and gave him a menacing look. Frank reached for another bottle and the guys nostrils flared.

"I swear I will toss this."

He was using anything as leverage. For the past five minutes he had been trying to make his way back over to his rifle. It was the first thing that was knocked out of his hands when the guy appeared out of nowhere. He figured the bar was empty. Sure it was locked up at the back and front, but the window was open on the second floor. He'd clambered up there using the fire escape. He just assumed someone had left it open. Though come to think of it, there was no rain on the floor and it had been raining hard over the previous four days. Once he made his way in, he darted down into the bar, hoping to have a pint of beer in peace and quiet. The only reason he was by himself was because he had gotten into an argument with Sal.

Sal hadn't been the same since he lost Gloria and Bailey. He turned inward and though he still answered when asked a question, for the most part he was quieter and more reserved than he used to be.

On the day after the house burned down, they had taken the bodies back into Clayton and had a funeral in the main cemetery. He didn't want to bury them on the island. Gloria wouldn't have approved, he said. As ludicrous as it sounded, Frank wasn't going to argue with him. He'd already distanced himself and Frank couldn't help but feel to blame for their deaths. He fully expected him to launch into some rant about how it was his fault. And sure enough, the very second they ended up in Gananqoue, that's what happened.

Frank had told Ella that it wasn't a good idea for Sal to go with them, but she figured that they would work out their differences if they spent a little time together.

That was a big mistake.

Frank's eyes flared as the guy in front of him roared. The bat came down hard on the bar and the nails punctured the wood, sending splitters flying. With his pulse beating hard, he scrambled back and lost his footing. He fell on his ass and shuffled back, trying to get up before he attacked again.

That had been close. Too close.

The man yanked on the bat but it wasn't coming out. Frank knew this was his chance. His feet barely touched the ground as he sprinted for the rifle but out the corner of his eye he saw the man reach for something. Before he made it within a few feet, he felt a hard smack to the side of his face and he collapsed on the ground. It didn't knock him out but it hurt like fuck! "What the hell!" he hollered as he glanced down and saw the same bottle of bourbon that he was going to toss at him. "Weren't you just complaining about me tossing shit at you?"

The guy didn't answer; he was already making his way over, though this time without a weapon. He didn't need the bat, as his arms were bats. Thick and veiny, with huge fists on the end, he swung them like battering rams. Each one struck Frank's face with bone crushing power. The next thing Frank knew, he was being lifted up into the air and tossed like a rag doll across the room. He landed on the other side of the bar and collided with a shelf of wine glasses. He groaned and winced in pain, looking down at the shards embedded in his hands. This guy was going to break his back at this rate. As fast as he wanted to move, it felt as if he had broken a rib.

Every breath was more difficult than the last.

"I bet you wish you hadn't entered now."

"Like I said, the window was open."

"I needed fresh air."

"How the hell was I supposed to know?"

"The signs."

"Oh, fuck the signs."

That was the wrong thing to say. The guy leaned over the bar and reached down and grabbed a hold of the back of Frank's collar. "Oh, come on man. I haven't stolen anything."

"But you were gonna!"

Hauled up like a crane lifting a rock, he slid Frank along the bar and launched him off the end. He nosedived into an old jukebox machine and it turned on and started playing the Beatles tune, All We Need Is Love.

The irony wasn't wasted.

Frank frowned, and clung to his bloody nose. "How the hell is that playing?" he muttered.

"Backup generator," the man said before bursting into

laughter.

* * *

Gabriel turned to Sal. "You know Frank was just trying to do his best, right?"

"Don't even go there, Gabriel."

"I'm just saying."

"Don't!" Sal rose from his seat and snagged up the last bottle of beer.

"I thought you said Frank was going to have that?"

"I lied."

He twisted the metal cap off the top and chugged it down as he wandered around the abandoned store. There were beds that had been flipped over, tables that had bullet holes in them and all manner of home décor scattered across the floor. Sal vaulted up on to what would have been the office desk and looked at all the paperwork. Receipts were everywhere. He picked one up. *Four thousand four hundred for a sofa set?* What a waste of money. Though Sal had earned a good salary as a psychiatrist, Gloria and him had never been ones to splurge on expensive items. It was all too vain and besides, where had it got people? The playing table had been leveled and now no one gave a shit about how they looked, what cars they drove or how big their house was. It meant nothing. All that was important was family, and besides Adrian, his family was gone. He ground his teeth and his mind drifted back to the argument with Frank.

Before they arrived in the main stretch of town, they had entered a home and Frank had picked up a photo of the family who once lived there. He'd tossed it down and the glass cracked.

"That's it, just toss it to one side, eh Frank?"

"What?"

Sal snorted. "Nothing."

Frank looked at him and Sal ran his hands over a ledge that had a thin layer of dust on it.

"What is it? Come on. Come out with it. You've been avoiding me since the funeral."

"You don't even know, do you?"

Frank looked at him with a look of confusion. "Enlighten

me."

Sal glared at the floor. "You know if you hadn't gone over there. Perhaps she would still be alive. Both of them."

Frank scowled. "Sal. Are you blaming me for their deaths?"

"If the boot fits."

He continued walking around the room pretending to not pay attention to his reactions, but he had been chomping at the bit to bring it up.

"I did what was needed to be done. I had no idea they would end up dead. If I thought for one moment they would have died, I would have done things differently."

"Really Frank? How? Huh?!"

"You self-righteous prick. I wasn't the only one that wanted to go over there. Wasn't it you who went down to the water, all prepared to swim across just so you could prove to Gloria you were a man?"

Rage filled in his chest and he swung at Frank, but Frank moved back and Sal lost his balance. He fell to the ground and felt like a complete chump. He couldn't even land a *punch.*

"You want to hit me? Come on, then. If that's what it takes. Then go ahead."

Sal rose up and brushed himself off. "You're not worth it."

The other two looked on. Gabriel's jaw hung as Sal walked away.

"Maybe we should search the town separately," Frank said.

The sound of a heavy object crashing jolted him back into the present moment. He glanced over to see that Zach had kicked over one of the large flat screen TV's.

"Sal!" Gabriel called out. "We should get back and find Frank."

"Yeah, we don't want him to enjoy himself too much," Zach muttered with a grin. That kid just loved to stir the pot.

* * *

Frank was beginning to feel like a rag doll. He'd been tossed, kicked and slammed into multiple walls. Sure, he managed to get in a few good shots, but that had only angered the guy even more. Every time he made a run for the rifle, the guy would block him.

He thought he would apply reverse psychology. Frank threw his hands up.

"Okay, you win. I'm done. Good job."

The guy stared at him for a second before a grin decorated his face.

"This isn't about winning. It's about making a statement." He shifted his weight on to his back leg and stared at Frank. "And I have this great idea of how I'm going to do it. You know truckers attach different items on the front of the grill? Bears and whatnot. Well, I'm going put your body outside the front of this bar. I'm thinking that should be a sign people will pay attention to."

Frank was down on one knee trying to get his breath. He'd caught sight of himself in the mirror behind the bar, blood streamed down his face.

"Are you kidding me?"

"Oh, I never say anything that I'm not prepared to

follow through with," the man said as he approached.

"Look, you can't be doing well cooped up in here all by yourself. Why not join us over on the island."

The man looked as if he was tempted by the offer. He moved over to the bar and twisted the lid off a bottle and for a brief few seconds, Frank thought he had him. He downed a gulp while keeping a good eye on him.

"I was never one for islands."

This wasn't going to end the way Frank hoped. Off to his right was a broken table leg. It had snapped after the guy must have decided he was going to reenact some of his favorite wrestling moves on Frank. Edging his hand over to it, the guy rushed at him. There was no time to think about what was the right thing to do. He'd given the guy plenty of chances to stop, but he'd obviously lost it.

Frank waited until he was practically on him when he snatched up that broken table leg and jammed it as hard as he could into the guy's solar plexus. He didn't let out a cry, only a few strained breaths as he staggered back, looking down at chunk of wood. Frank didn't waste a second. He was up and across the room to grab his rifle, fully expecting the guy to withdraw the leg and follow through with another attack.

He didn't.

As he scooped up the rifle, he heard the guy crash behind him. Frank looked at him and shook his head.

"It didn't have to be this way."

The guy gurgled, spluttered, and blood trailed out of his mouth before he breathed his last breath.

Chapter 2

As she lay on her back, Kate observed the world as it forced its way back in. For a second, she wondered why she couldn't draw a breath, then quickly became more troubled by the pain coursing through her body. All she could do was lay still, blinking and feeling the agonizing throb.

From nearby she heard the sound of a body rush by, boots stamping the ground like an army of men, and yet it was only one person. The culprit that had shot her. As hard as she tried to concentrate and regain her ability to move, everything was jumbled up.

Was he talking to her? It was definitely a male voice. Where was it coming from? It seemed to be telling her to hold on.

At the same time, the world around her slowly came back into view. Her focus sharpened, sounds became clear, and the taste of iron flooded her mouth. She blinked hard, turned her head, and was confronted by a figure looming over her. It was the security guard, Jake Roberts.

"Mrs. Talbot. Mrs. Talbot. Can you hear me?"

She gave a nod while trying to search for words. She could feel pressure being applied to her right shoulder. The pain was intense beyond anything she had felt before. It was throbbing and pulsating up and down her arm.

"What happened?"

"Listen, don't worry about that, you're going to feel some pressure in your arm, I'm going to raise it above your head. We need to get some elevation on this. You're lucky; it looks like the bullet went straight through. You're going to have one gnarly scar but you'll live." He stared into her eyes and then continued. "Do you have any bandages?"

Just as she was about to reply he raised her arm and she let out a blood-curdling cry. Kate had never been one for pain. Frank used to laugh when she stubbed her toe and screamed bloody murder. Others might have just sworn, but she nearly shattered windows with her high-pitched howl. With all the noise she made, Frank was certain that the neighbors would think that he was beating her.

"Uh," she tried to register what he was saying, but the pain was pushing out any and all logical thoughts. She swallowed hard and tried to get up, but he told her to stay where she was.

"I'll be right back."

Fear overtook her and she wanted to cry out and tell him to stay. Was the intruder still in the apartment? But he rushed off. She could hear rifling in the cupboards, then a drawer being pulled out, a tap being turned on, and then he returned.

"Okay. Okay. Um."

She could tell he was panicking. This wasn't normal and he obviously hadn't been in a situation like this before.

"Do you know what you're doing?"

He let out a nervous chuckle. "Would you feel more

relaxed if I said, yes?"

That wasn't the answer she was hoping for. She attempted to get up, thinking that she better get to a hospital while she was still conscious, but he reassured her that he knew what he was doing, as he'd originally tried to become a medic before shifting over into security.

"So, tell me again, why did you change careers?"

"Oh, I never graduated."

"Did you get bored?"

"No, I failed the testing."

She looked at him and he gave a smirk. "Listen up, if there was any rapid swelling, that would indicate you have internal bleeding or a bone has been shattered. But, so far so good."

"So far so good? How's it look?" she tried to see but he turned her head back towards him.

"Probably best not to look at it. I've seen folks faint from the sight of blood. Right now I'm going to keep some pressure on this and make sure the bleeding stops."

"And if it doesn't?"

"I'll press on the brachial artery."

"The what?"

"It's just below your armpit."

She gave a slight nod.

"And if that doesn't slow it down?"

"I'll apply pressure nearer the heart."

"And…"

"Mrs. Talbot. Relax. It's going to be okay."

"Call me Kate."

He nodded.

A tear streamed out the corner of her eye. She was scared to die and if she was going to leave this world, she didn't want to do it before telling Ella that she loved her. Jake continued to apply pressure, removing what appeared to be one of her best cloths and checking the wound every so often.

"What if the bullet had become lodged?"

"It hasn't."

"But if it had?"

He shook his head. "There are lots of military folk out

there that live with shrapnel in their bodies. Unless you end up with some infection, the body is quite resilient and it can adapt to having metal inside it without any serious issue. It all comes down to the situation and if you can pull it out safely without causing further blood loss. Some bullets can end up corking up a blood vessel and you wouldn't want to yank it out."

Kate stared at his dark uniform. On his shoulder was a patch with a white eagle, the American flag on a shield and the words: *Angel Security. We'll Watch Over You.* She snorted and then groaned and began a coughing fit.

"You okay?"

"Yeah, I was just admiring the patch on your shoulder. The irony."

He glanced at it and smiled. "Oh right, yeah. I'm a real angel."

They both laughed a little until Kate winced again. Jake was a good looking guy, a little on the young side for her, but nevertheless he had handsome features. A chiseled jaw, short, dark, wavy hair and dark eyes.

"What happened to the intruder?"

"I did a quick sweep of the apartment, he was gone by the time I got here. You must have spooked him. We have a busted back entrance on the building, I've been trying to keep them out, but they've been getting in. They're like rats."

"Desperation will do that."

"You work for the CDC, right?"

"Yeah."

He took another look at her wound, dabbed some water around it and dried it off, then changed over to a new cloth.

"So what's the verdict, are we royally screwed?"

"That about sums it up."

He shook his head and scoffed. "You know, I never thought that it would end this way."

"No?"

"I was certain that North Korea or Russia would fire a nuclear warhead at us. Crazy, isn't it? To think that we all live on the same ball of dirt and yet we all act like kids in a playground."

"In what way?"

"Cliques. Our country. Our God. Our rules. It's like we can't stand the thought that perhaps we are wrong. You know… about it all. Oh no, that doesn't even factor into it. Everyone has to protect their piece of the pie."

"It's human nature, Jake. In our need to be valued we maximize ourselves and minimize others."

"But that doesn't make it right, does it?"

"I guess not." She glanced over and caught sight of the bloody cloth. "You think you can get me a drink of water? There should be some bottles under the sink, unless they were taken."

"Yeah, hold on to this." He placed her hand on the wound and she ground her teeth. It was burning and her arm was throbbing like mad. She called out to him. "If we can get back to the CDC building, there are medical supplies we could use to treat this."

"You up to it?" he said returning with a bottle of water.

"No choice." She pulled off the cloth to get a better look at it. It was a grim sight of torn flesh and a small hole. She quickly covered it back up and then took the bottle from Jake. He crouched down, swapped out the old cloth with a new one, and then took a piece of cloth and gently tied off the wound. "Is that my tablecloth?"

He grinned. "Yeah, I bet you never thought you would wind up using it like this."

"There are a lot of things I never thought I would see."

He helped her up to her feet. She was a little wobbly so she took a moment to lean against the wall.

"Any other residents still here?"

"Several. I guess most people think this is going to pass."

She nodded slightly. "I did, too." She pushed away from the wall and kept one hand on her wound to keep pressure on it.

"You got a vehicle?"

"Yeah."

Jake looked around as if he was searching for

something. "Look, if I grab a bag, you can tell me what you want in it, and I'll take you over to the CDC."

"I can drive."

"Like hell you can."

He wandered up the winding stairs that led to the second level.

"What about your job?"

Jake leaned over the balcony style glass enclosure. Kate craned her head to see what he was doing. "If you had asked me that before the lights went out, and some raving lunatic opened fire on you, I would have said I needed it. But hell no, they don't pay me enough to put up with this bullshit."

Her lip curled up at the corner. She began shouting out a few things that she wanted to take with her and where he could find them. Jake went back and forth as she continued down the list in her mind.

"You do know how big this bag is right? We aren't going to be able to lug a suitcase out of here."

"Okay dump the shoes, the coats."

By the time he had everything inside the bag, he'd made her throw out two thirds of what she had originally wanted. She had to think logically about this. While she could fill up the car with all manner of possessions, she just needed the basics. When Jake came down holding the duffel bag, she recalled the day that she left Frank.

It had been one hell of a fight the night before. That was the problem. They were either loving towards each other or plain bat shit crazy. There was never an in-between and in all honesty, it was exhausting. She'd never felt scared around Frank. He wasn't the kind of man to raise a fist, but she had become tired of arguing over the smallest things. If asked, she wouldn't even be able to recall most of the crap they argued over. It was insignificant things but usually related to his phobia.

The worst part about it all was Ella was stuck in the middle. She had to hear them fighting. Kate had once found her tucked away in her cupboard, curled up in a ball with her hands over her ears. She didn't understand. Kids rarely did until they got older. Life wasn't just black and white, but a whole array of colors in between and trying to find the words to explain was near impossible.

Of course she knew it wasn't all Frank's fault. She was as stubborn as him. Selfish even. But anyone in her shoes would have been. It wasn't like she was married a year and then upped and walked out on him. They had a good marriage, a long one, but as the years wore on, his illness slowly wore her down. She'd forgotten who she was before it all. Many of the simple pleasures of life had slipped through her grasp in her attempt to ensure that the place was always clean, always sanitary, and always just right.

"You okay, Mrs. Talbot?" Jake asked.

She blinked. "Yes."

"Ready to go, then?"

She nodded and they ventured out into the dark corridor towards the stairwell. Her eyes scanned back and forth. Even though Jake was carrying a handgun, she didn't feel safe. It was hard to feel safe now.

When they managed to make it into the underground

parking lot, she was shocked to find her vehicle had been stolen.

"You've got to be joking!"

Jake placed the bag on the ground. "I guess we are lugging it out of here."

"That's a long walk."

The day was just getting worse by the minute. Trapped in an elevator, shot in the arm, vehicle stolen. Could anything else go wrong? She didn't even want to think about it.

Chapter 3

A bright light shone in Frank's eyes as he emerged from the bar, carrying a bag full of alcohol. He raised a hand. Bruised, cut and distraught by his encounter with the guy who wouldn't take no for an answer, he was greeted by the familiar sound of Gabriel's voice.

"Frank!"

Frank squinted, trying to allow his eyes to adjust after they lowered the flashlight.

"What the hell happened to you?" Zach said, staring past him as if expecting to see a mob. But it wasn't a mob that had done this, just one man. A crazy asshole, but nevertheless, just one man. Gabriel immediately handed him a rag to wipe his face, but the blood had already dried.

"Just a bar brawl."

"Are they still in there?"

"They? Him you mean?"

Frank noted that Sal wasn't saying anything. He figured he was relishing the fact that Frank had got his ass kicked and had come close to death.

"Here, let me take those," Zach said, stepping forward to take the heavy bag. The bottles clinked inside as the made their way back to the marina following King Street East. It was a fair hike that had taken them around fifteen minutes when they arrived earlier that afternoon.

"Did you find anything of value?" Frank asked.

"Not much. Some cans of food, but I'm thinking we should check out that grocery store on the way back through. You know Metro," Zach said.

"I already told you, there isn't going to be anything left. That would have been one of the first places people hit."

"Well, can we at least check it out?"

Sal sighed and walked ahead.

"How's he been?" Frank asked Gabriel.

"You know. The same. He avoids any attempt at talking about it. You doing okay?"

"Yeah, I'm just giving him a wide berth for a while. I'm sure he'll come around. It's not easy losing a wife and child."

The truth was he didn't fully understand what Sal was going through. He'd only ever known the threat of losing Ella. When it came down to it, he wasn't sure how he would react. Since they had argued earlier that day he had chewed over what Sal had said. Was he to blame? Was that how it would be now? That every death that occurred from now on, someone would get blamed for saying the wrong thing, doing the wrong thing? He had run through every possible scenario that he could have taken and it didn't matter. It would have still come down to Butch attacking the island, of that he was sure.

A huge red and white metro sign loomed up ahead as they entered the empty parking lot. Across the street were several clapboard homes. Nothing special. Shopping carts littered the lot, some turned over on their sides. When they reached the main doors, they found the glass had been smashed in. That was one of the reasons why they didn't check it the first time around. Sal assumed that all the goods would have been scavenged. He was the first one in the door. He entered without a second of hesitation. If Frank wasn't mistaken, he almost looked as if he had a death wish. Gabriel called out to remind him to be cautious, but he didn't respond. He just disappeared into the darkness.

Once they made their way inside, the smell of rotting vegetables was rancid. It reminded Frank of the days Kate would leave the broccoli out on the side and in the heat of summer it would spoil.

Frank shouldered his rifle as he moved quietly into the store. After the last surprise he got at the bar, he wasn't taking any chances. People were losing their shit with the virus, but since the blackout, craziness had been jacked up to a whole new level.

"Sal, hold up!"

He turned around and even though it was dark, and the light from his flashlight wasn't on his face, Frank could see him glaring at him in the glow of yellow. They decided to split up; Zach would go with Sal and Gabriel would stick with Frank. They moved down the aisles that were clogged with what remained, which was barely anything. Their eyes drifted over the barren shelves. Occasionally, Gabriel would scoop up a product only to toss it back down. Just like the residents in Clayton, people had taken matters into their own hands. They spent close to ten minutes going up and down aisles hoping to find something, but there wasn't even a can of beans.

"Satisfied, can we go now?" Sal said like an all-knowing brat. Frank shook his head and wandered into the stock area. Brown boxes were strewn all over the ground. He had to kick them out of the way just to get through. Someone had routed through every inch of the place. His flashlight swept over crates, then he spotted something. He focused his light in on what looked like... before he could get a clear shot, it moved, darting across the room. Both Gabriel and him went on the alert, keeping their backs close to each other and turning ever so slightly. Again, the silhouette of a dark form shot into view, then vanished behind a stack of pallets.

Gabriel fired a round and it ricocheted off the side of the metal enclosure, causing golden sparks to erupt. They hit the ground.

"Careful, you idiot. You'll get us both killed."

"How the hell was I supposed to know it was metal? It's so dark in here."

Frank rose from his feet and hollered. "Come on out."

No sooner had he said that when Gabriel let out a cry and collapsed to the ground.

Frank bent at the waist over him. "What happened?"

"Something hit me in the back of the legs."

"What?"

He had barely spat the words from his mouth when he felt the sting of pain as someone struck him across the knee with what felt like a block of wood. He crumbled to his side, hollering in agony while at the same time sweeping his gun around in the darkness. Frank shuffled over to a shelving unit. In the distance he could hear Zach calling out to him.

"What's going on?"

Frank frantically scanned the area before him, trying to make sense of what had just happened. One hand held his gun; the other rubbed the side of his knee. Again, there was movement off to his right, this time he fired without thought to the rebounding rounds. Fortunately it must have embedded in some of the packaging, as no sparks lit up the place.

Sal and Zach rushed around the corner out of breath and Frank nearly shot them. He lowered his weapon. Zach dropped down beside him and started checking for blood.

"Something is out there."

Both of them went into defense mode and positioned themselves either side of Frank and Gabriel. Their rifles swept back and forth. It was silent inside the stock area. Each of them listened intently for movement — then it happened — the sound of feet moving fast in their direction. Whoever it was, they weren't trying to escape;

they were hell bent on pummeling them. Zach fired off a round and once again sparks ignited. This time Frank caught sight of the figure. Frank gestured with his hands for Zach to go one way, while Sal and him would go the other. Gabriel would stay put. As Frank and Sal circled around the shelving unit, they heard the figure run the other way, straight into Zach. What ensued shortly after was the sound of a kid yelling for him to let go.

"Get off!"

"You are a wiggly bastard."

By the time they made their way down to Zach, they found that he had turned the kid upside down and was gripping them by the pants. Sal shone his light on the kid's face and both of them squinted.

It was just a girl.

She couldn't have been more than ten years of age.

"Zach, put her down," Sal said, stepping forward to get a better look. Zach kept a firm grip on her collar to make sure she didn't bolt. He looked like he was trying to hold back a ferocious wild cat; she was flailing her arms and legs and uttering threats as if she honestly believed she could stand a chance. They shone the light over her and from what Frank could tell, she had dark hair, blue eyes, her face was dirty and the clothes looked as if she had spent a long time in some dusty corner.

"Settle down. What's your name?"

She didn't reply, but just stared.

"Look, I know you're scared, but we aren't going to harm you."

"That's what the last group said," she muttered in a low voice.

"How many other people have you crippled?" Gabriel said, hobbling around the corner.

Sal placed his weapon down and put his hands up. "Seriously, what's your name?"

Reluctantly she replied, "Eva."

"And where are you parents, Eva?"

"Dead." She said it so matter of factly and with so little emotion that it made Frank wonder what her mental state was like. What had she seen? But better question, was she infected? His eyes widened.

"Zach. You might want to back up."

"No way, keep a good hold on her. She is liable to knee cap you," Gabriel muttered while leaning against a shelving unit.

"Are you infected?" Sal asked. He was still a good distance away.

"Do I look infected?" she shot back with a sarcastic grin on her face. That was all it took for Frank to start questioning her.

"How long have you been in here?"

"Since the beginning. After my parents died, I came here to find food."

"And there was none, right?" Zach muttered.

"No. There was food here. It was closed but I got in through a back window."

"That just happened to be open?" Gabriel asked.

She scoffed. "No, I broke it. Why would they leave a window open?" She tutted as if she was dealing with imbeciles.

"So, where's the food now?"

She didn't answer.

"Come on, if you've been here all this time, you couldn't have survived on the rats."

They'd seen a few on the way in. It was to be expected. With a busted entrance it wouldn't take long before critters showed up. Sal obviously picked up on her hesitation and posed the question a different way.

"Eva, we are staying on an island not far from here. There are others kids your age there. Would you like to come with us? They'll be other kids you can play with."

She let out a laugh. "I'm eleven, not five. I gave up finger painting years ago."

Frank chuckled, and Sal glared at him.

"Okay, my mistake, but it's safer than here."

"I can look after myself. I've done okay so far. Besides, you might be perverts. My parents always told me to watch out for perverts and you seem to match the description pretty well."

Gabriel stifled a laugh.

She was acting more mature than what he'd expected. Frank glanced back out through the plastic that separated the storage area from the rest of the store. He didn't want to stay in there any longer than they needed.

"Listen up kid. If you like staying here, then suit yourself, but there is a warm bed back where we are, a fireplace, real food and people who might actually protect you. Your decision. As for us, we're leaving now."

Frank turned and ambled over to the exit. Sal called out to him.

"Frank. Frank!"

When Frank didn't respond, he caught up with him and caught hold of his arm."

"We can't leave her here."

"Seems to be doing fine to me," Frank said in a loud enough voice that she would hear.

"Jesus, Frank, don't you have a heart?"

Frank leaned in and whispered. "Just run with me on this."

Sal screwed up his face and it took him a few seconds

to clue in. "Oh. Right. Yeah," he sniffed. "Yeah, let's leave her here. I'm sure she enjoys the company of rats and random lunatics who show up. Come on fellas, let's go. Nothing here of value."

The other two were confused of course, but that was the whole point. Sal and Frank made their way out of the storage area and quickly Gabriel caught up.

"Guys?" he thumbed over his shoulder. "Are we really going to do this?"

"Yep. It's a pity! But some people don't like to be helped," Frank said in his loudest voice. "Let's go. I hear we're having chicken tonight."

Frank grinned, and then went stone faced the moment Sal looked at him.

Gabriel cast a glance over his shoulder but trudged on with them. They hadn't made it to the cash out tills when they heard her call out to them.

"I know where you can find some food, that is, if that warm bed is still available?"

They all stopped and turned back. She was standing at

the end of the aisle, holding on to a small bag. A weak smile spread across Sal's face.

"Lead the way," Frank said, making his way back down to her. Eva led them back into the storage area, through a series of corridors and then stopped to pry off a large vent cover. She squeezed inside and told them to wait there. The sound of thin metal clanging around could be heard as she ferreted her way down the vent that was only big enough for a small child. Then there was silence.

"You think this is a good idea? I mean, bringing her back without checking to see if she's infected?"

"We'll keep our distance and place her in isolation for twenty-four hours."

"Isolation?" Sal asked, making it sound as if Frank wanted to toss her in a dungeon.

"Yeah Sal. Isolation. I'm sure she won't be the last person we come across. We are going to need somewhere where folks can stay until we can determine if they're clear. I'm thinking a couple of the houses on the east side can be used. It's only for twenty-four hours. They'll still be fed, given a bed and the essentials, but we need to be cautious."

"I think we are beyond that," Zach said. Each of them had been keeping their distance from him. He was the only one that had come in contact with her.

"Well, look at this way, Zach, you'll get to look after her for a day as you're going in there when we get back," Gabriel said.

"Are you joking? Frank?"

Sal piped up. "He's right, Zach. You might be infected."

Zach's shoulders sunk and he leaned back against the wall, looking despondent. The fact was they had to be more cautious and mindful of the virus. So far they had managed to dodge a few dubious events, but with every passing day the odds were being stacked against them.

"You alive in there?" Gabriel shouted. His voice echoed off the tin enclosure. A few minutes more and they heard the sound of Eva heading back. It sounded as if she was sliding a large box. When she reemerged, she pushed out a small burlap bag and then opened it. It was filled with cans of food. All kinds of beans, potatoes, tomatoes, soup, tuna, chili, peaches, corn, peas, ravioli and more.

"How did you get all this?"

She looked real proud of herself. "I figured it would be only a matter of time before everyone lost their head. Besides, my uncle worked here. I'd been here enough times to know that they store a lot of items in the back of the trucks. When I got here, it was still all there. I simply gathered a whole bunch of it and stuffed it into bags and filled up the vents. I figured no one would go looking for it in there. The rest of the rooms in this place have all been torn apart."

"Smart kid," Sal said. Frank noticed the way he was looking at her. While she didn't resemble Bailey, she was about the same height and age.

"So there's more?" Zach asked inquisitively. She nodded.

"How many bags?"

She shrugged. "I lost count."

Gabriel let out a loud, "Yes!" and fist pumped the air. Over the course of the next fifteen to twenty minutes, they formed a line and brought each of the bags out. By the time they had them all, it was up in the range of thirty three. They stood a short distance away just reveling at the sight of what few others would ever see again.

"Only one problem."

"What's that?" Frank said with a grin on his face.

"How we going lug all of this out of here?"

Just as he said that, Eva disappeared back into the vent. They assumed she was going to collect some of her personal belongings. When her head poked out, she dangled a pair of keys.

"Anyone know how to drive a truck?"

Her face beamed, as did Sal's. It had been one of the few times that Frank had seen him smile since losing Gloria and Bailey. Perhaps this kid would help draw him back to his old self. Or maybe it would remind him again of what he'd lost.

It was a slow process hauling the bags to the loading dock. There were three huge trucks. Zach was curious as to why no one had taken them. Obviously they could have been hot-wired, but few people knew how to do that and those who could would have chosen something a little bit easier to drive. These suckers were massive.

They piled all of the bags into the back, along with Eva and Zach, then brought the steel doors down and locked it into place.

"Maybe things are looking up," Gabriel muttered as they pulled out of the lot, and headed for the marina.

What they weren't aware of was that several locals were watching.

They were hungry. Desperate. And ready to kill if need be.

Chapter 4

Chester Grayson raised his double barrel shotgun as the grouse took flight. As smooth as ice, he slowly squeezed the trigger and released a round. A smattering of feathers filled the air as the plump bird dropped to the earth.

"Go get it, boy," he said to Riley, his yellow lab. The dog shot off in the direction of the animal and Chester looked off to his left and right to see how his cousins were doing. He'd spent the early part of his teen years in Frank E. Jadwin State Park. Back then, it was less about hunting and more about getting drunk, getting laid and get stoned. Of course, he chose to keep that information out of his police interview. Never in his worst nightmares did he imagine he would find himself having to hunt to survive. It was something they did a few times a year, and they never took it seriously. It was just a means of unwinding and unloading his pent up frustration, and...

in many ways it worked.

But not now.

Not a single day had passed that he hadn't thought about Talbot.

It wasn't just the fact that he had set ablaze to his cruiser. He didn't give a fuck about that. It was the brazen nature of what he had done that irked him. That the guy had the nerve to stroll back into his town and piss in his face. It was defiant. Had he caught him, he would have knocked him down and given him one hell of a beating. Apocalypse or not — that shit didn't fly.

His dog rushed back with the grouse in its jaws. It dropped it at his feet and he patted him on the head. Hell, even his dog knew his place, but Talbot, now that guy needed someone to demonstrate that there were consequences to his actions.

"How many you got, Chester?" Bobby asked.

"Two so far. You?"

"One."

"One? After three hours out here?"

He shrugged and sneered, "You didn't do much better yesterday."

"I'm starting to think we should only eat what we kill, which means I get two tonight and you two fuckers can have whatever you haul back."

"Oh, come on Chester," Pat griped.

All of them were dressed in typical hunting gear with bright orange ball caps. That was mandatory for Chester. A few years back, he nearly got his head shot off by some asshole that thought he was a deer. He sure regretted that slip of the finger.

Chester dropped his chin. "I'm heading back."

"But we're not done."

"I am," he said, walking backwards and scowling at them.

He heard Sawyer grumble and ask the others what was up his ass. After the town of Lowville when to shits and people started dropping like flies, he knew it was time to get the hell out of there. They didn't have to gather much up as the hunting cottage was already stocked up for the worst-case scenario. Could they be called preppers? He didn't like to think of himself that way. It invoked images of paranoid people, and he sure as hell wasn't one of them.

It was a twenty-minute hike through the state park back to the cottage. He left the truck with the others so he could have time to think. Chester stuffed some fresh chewing tobacco behind his gum and got his jaw working on it. Lugging the rifle over his shoulder he pressed on, keeping his eyes open for any other survivors. They had come across a few of them, and in his usual fashion, he made it crystal clear that if they wandered into his territory they would spit blood. The last thing he needed was another group eating his food supply; they barely had enough as it was. Pat had miscalculated the amount of food required to get them through a year. It turned out they only had enough for six months.

The state forest they were in was one of the biggest in upstate New York, clocking in at over 20,000 acres. It provided more than enough wildlife that they could live on after their supplies dried up. The brush was full of ponds and wetlands. Their cottage was just on the south side, closer to the edge of the forest and only thirty minutes from Lowville. The cottage was meant to be a retreat for the boys, a place they could all use in the summer. It wasn't big but it was remote enough, and shielded from prying eyes by clusters of conifer forest. Still, after two months of being there he was beginning to get cabin fever and go a little stir crazy.

Finally, when Chester reached the cottage he found Tex and Roy outside on the porch. They had their feet up and were smoking and drinking beer. Both had AR-15s beside them. Chester had told them to stay behind to protect the goods. So far they hadn't had anyone traipse through the property, but it wouldn't be long before someone did and he wanted to make damn sure they didn't steal his shit. There were nine of them. Tex, Roy, Sawyer, James, Bobby, Pat. A couple of them children and were married. It had been tough trying to convince them to head to the cottage. They were all gung-ho when there was no pandemic. Everyone had ideas about how they would survive and yet when it came down to it, besides Bobby, Pat and Sawyer, the rest were reluctant to come unless they brought their wives. That was a problem, and the real reason why they would only have six months of supplies. Of course, Pat had an excuse.

"I didn't know how many were going to be there," he'd said. Somewhere in his tiny little head he expected there only to be four of them.

As Chester entered the clearing in front of the cottage, he glanced at Tex and Roy.

"Aren't you guys meant to be circling the perimeter?"

"You need to ease up pal, if anyone is going to hit this place they have to make it through the front entrance. There is no back door."

Chester shifted his weight from one foot to the other. "Is that so?"

They nodded and took another swig of their drink.

"And how do you suppose you're going to survive if someone creeps up the side of the house and puts a slug in your head?"

"Wouldn't happen," Tex said confidently. He made a gesture to either side of the house where he had attached two car mirrors. "Trust us, we can see everything."

Chester brought up the muzzle of rifle in one smooth motion and pointed at them. "Do you see this?"

Tex tossed Roy a nervous look.

"Now tell me, how are you going to defend this house when the DAMN GUNS ARE BESIDE YOU!" he yelled in anger before unloading a round in the dirt. They jumped to their feet, tossed the beer cans and snatched up their rifles and wandered off to circle the area. He shook his head and went in to cottage, wondering if their stupidity was infectious.

* * *

Inside, Tex's grandmother, Martha, was busy stirring the contents of a pot that was placed over the fireplace. With the power out, they generally cooked outside, but if the weather looked as if it was threatening rain, they'd just toss a grill over the cottage fireplace.

"You really shouldn't be so hard on them, Chester."

"You won't be saying that when some asshole bursts in here and tries to kills you."

She shook her head. Martha had never been interested in survival skills. In her mind, it was overrated. She was in the group that thought that society would never buckle under the strain of a virus, a nuclear war or some act of God. Sure, Chester wasn't exactly convinced that the world would go to hell, but he wasn't stupid. He paid insurance for a reason. Having a place to retreat to that was stocked up with the bare essentials was just wisdom. There were countless Americans that owned cottages. How hard would it have been to create a stockroom full of supplies? Hell, at the bare minimum they could invest a few hundred dollars and still be more prepared than the average Joe.

"Anyway, you want some stew?"

"I've been stewing enough."

"You need to let it go, Chester. That was then, this is now. Focus on getting through the next year."

"I am, woman."

She tutted and came over and filled his bowl with some beef stew. Steam spiraled up and he inhaled its goodness. Martha had become almost like a mother to them all. She seemed to thrive on making sure that all of them were eating enough, drinking enough and keeping the place sanitary. When she wasn't cooking, she was cleaning or dealing with laundry. Beatrix, Tex's wife, was completely different. She'd made it clear right from the get-go that she wasn't going to be cleaning up their shit. She was a fire cracker that had bigger balls than Tex.

"Where's Beatrix?"

"Hunting."

Chester put his spoon down. "But we told her to stay here."

"Yeah, best of luck with that. You can't be telling her what to do, she has a mind of her own."

He grunted and continued spooning in mouthfuls of the delicious stew. One thing for sure, with Martha around the food would at least taste good. She was a whiz in the kitchen and she sure knew how to make bland food explode in the mouth.

"Listen, I'm thinking of heading north."

"You don't listen, do you?"

"I'm a grown ass man, Martha."

She nodded with a look of disbelief. "So what do you think you're going to achieve going up there and raising hell? Huh?"

"Get my respect back."

She sighed. "Didn't Robbie ever teach you when to quit?"

Robbie was his old man; he'd died five years ago from liver disease. He'd practically poisoned himself to death with the liquor. When he was alive and not drunk, which was very rarely, he was a good man. The kind of father that any kid would look up to; he just had a few flaws. The main one being alcoholism. Chester never did find out why he drank so much, he just avoided him on the bad days.

"He taught me a lot."

"And you think he would have approved?"

Chester looked at Martha and for a brief moment he considered that perhaps he would have. Robbie was never one for backing down from a fight. His bar fights had become legendary in Lowville. Maybe somewhere in his past he had inherited that 'fuck 'em all' attitude or perhaps it was just the fact that he still saw himself as a man of the law — and under any other conditions, Talbot would have been locked up by now for what he had done.

"Chester!" a voice called out, he couldn't discern who it was initially, then they shouted again. Chester shot up, grabbed his rifle and rushed towards the door. He was ready for war and by the sounds of yelling going on outside, he fully expected to find the others embroiled in some exchange of gunfire. Instead, when he threw the door open, he found Bobby and Sawyer carrying Pat. He had one foot up and was wincing in pain.

"Please tell me you did not shoot yourself in the foot."

"The gun went off and…" he grimaced and tried to

find the words to continue but his face was a picture of agony. Chester walked back inside to finish his lunch with even more resolve to follow through on what he had planned for Talbot.

* * *

The journey from Atlanta to Clayton, New York wasn't one for the faint hearted. No one in their right mind drove the long sixteen to eighteen hour trip even when all was well in the world.

The previous evening they had headed over to the CDC and used what they could to treat the wound. It wasn't infected, but she'd have to keep a close eye on it. The first thing on the agenda for the day was locating a vehicle. Getting beyond the barricades was now the easy part. Government employees had abandoned their posts after the virus had spread far beyond the confines that they had quarantined.

Now everyone was fighting to stay alive.

They filled a bag with meds and whatever they could manage to carry and then donned N-95 masks, biohazard suits, and goggles before leaving. Outside, it was dark. Carrying nothing more than a Glock for protection, they aimed to put in as many miles as they could before it was daylight.

"Do you think he'll lend the vehicle?" Kate asked.

They had already been on the road for close to three hours heading for the outskirts of Atlanta. Jake was lugging a backpack over his shoulder. Every few feet he would shift it back up and readjust it.

"Maybe. I hope."

Kate mumbled to herself. She hadn't been in a very talkative mood. Her mind was preoccupied by pain and the danger that lurked ahead. The country had pretty much been turned on its head. It was wild and desolate as people tried to avoid contact. The thought gave her an idea.

"Remind me when we get to your grandfather's house to find a marker pen."

"You want to write your will?"

She chuckled. "Nope. I'm going to scribble a mustache

on your face in the night."

That wasn't what she wanted it for, but she was doing her best to stay positive in a dire situation.

"Anyway, as I was saying." This guy could talk the ear off a donkey, he hadn't shut up since they left the apartment block. "Where was I?"

"The power."

"Yeah, makes you wonder, doesn't it? Are we to assume that the grid just shut down? Or do you think someone destroyed it by accident?"

"You do ask the strangest questions. All we know is there is no power. It's troubling, but so is being stuck out here with the potential of getting infected."

Jake took out his gun and showed it to her. "You ever fired a weapon before?"

"My ex-husband was in the military."

"And?"

She scuffed her feet along the road as they passed burnt out vehicles. A few large blackbirds pecked at the eye sockets of some unlucky individual. From human to animal, the virus would spread even further afield. What little hope was there for humanity? How the hell could anyone come back from this? For all the money that had been spent on black budget projects, and yet they couldn't see this coming. Different strains of bad bacteria were immune to the latest antibiotics, and viruses, well, they couldn't even be treated by them. Years gone by, people would have to just ride it out. But no one was riding this one out. It was a one-way ticket to death's door.

Jake had said that his grandfather didn't live too far, but after three hours of trudging in the blazing heat she was starting to think that he was delirious and suffering from a mild case of sun stroke.

They arrived in Tucker, a small town in Georgia, a little after one that afternoon. A sign displaying the population of over 27,000 had been sprayed with red paint to change the number to zero. She didn't dwell on it. Some adolescent probably did it long before the virus had hit, at least she hoped. They hadn't seen many people on the roads.

When they arrived at a road called Regency Drive, they were sweating and thirsty. Because the power was off, it meant there'd be no water being pumped through the system, so they were living on a hope and a prayer that his grandfather would have bottled water, something Jake didn't seem too convinced about.

They sauntered up to the door and Jake fished around in his jacket for a key.

"He gave you a key to his place?"

"I rent a room out the back. After my girlfriend booted me out I needed a place to stay, and well, he was kind enough to help me out."

Jake shouldered the door but it appeared to be jammed. He took a few more stabs at it before he was able to see what was jamming the door. Peering in the gap that he'd managed to make, he stepped back and reached for his nose. It was the smell of death seeping out. Behind the door was a body.

They circled around back and Jake used his elbow to

shatter the glass on the rear door. As soon as they entered they knew it wasn't good. It stunk to high heaven. The rancid smell of rotten flesh lingered, as did the sound of flies buzzing. Jake moved slowly into the corridor to get a better look. He squeezed his eyes shut at the sight of his grandfather's corpse. The guy must have become infected and had tried to get his coat on and leave to get medical help, but he never made it. He'd collapsed still clasping a set of car keys in his hand.

Jake stumbled back into the kitchen and Kate told him not to touch anything. Even though they were fully clothed in biohazard gear, the chance of them contracting was still high.

"You going to be okay?" Kate asked, noticing that Jake's eyes were welling up with tears. He leaned against the wall and slumped down, staring at the oven.

"What about your grandmother?"

"She died six years ago."

Ten minutes passed without any word spoken.

"You couldn't have prevented it."

He nodded. "I just wish I was here to have helped him. To think that he died alone." He slapped a broom that was perched against the wall beside him.

"We come into this world alone, and we go out of it alone."

Kate was at a loss for what to say. She knew that sticking around wasn't going to do him any good, never mind the glaring fact that they were more likely to contract the virus if they continued to remain inside for any length of time. His grandfather's saliva, sweat or blood could have been on anything. She had flashbacks of Tom. He'd taken every precaution and yet he still wound up dead.

"That marker pen?" she asked, trying to take his mind off his grandfather.

"Check that second drawer."

After finding one, Kate took a moment to route through the recycling and pull out a couple pieces of cardboard.

"What are you doing there?"

"You'll see."

When she turned around, Jake squinted at the sign and then laughed.

"I thought we could wear them around our necks as a deterrent."

On each of the piece of cardboard was the word. 'I'M INFECTED.'

"Are you serious?"

"Why not? No one is going to come within a mile of us."

"Those signs will probably get us shot. For someone who works for the CDC, you're not that smart."

She frowned and then he backtracked. "That came out wrong. I mean..."

Kate just shrugged it off. "Let's just get the vehicle and get out."

"Yeah, easier said than done. The keys are in his hand."

"You don't have another set?"

"No, that car was his baby. He restored it. There's no

way on God's green earth he would have let anyone drive it."

"But you said he would have a vehicle."

"And he does. I couldn't guarantee he was going to let us use it."

She shook her head for a second, then figured that perhaps the reason they visited his grandfather was more about checking up on his wellbeing than it was about the vehicle. Jake sniffed hard and hauled himself up and entered the corridor again. He hesitated.

"We can sanitize the keys, and we have some more gloves for you to change into."

She pulled off her backpack and held out a pair of gloves.

He shrugged. "I don't care."

With that said, he approached his grandfather, stooped over him and pulled the keys from his hand. If he weren't already wearing a pair of gloves, she would have been furious. Kate heard him mutter something about rest in peace before he opened the garage door.

He was about to enter when Kate spoke up.

"Jake, we need to sanitize the keys."

He nodded and returned to the kitchen. Kate spent a few minutes going through the process of sanitizing using a few bottles from the CDC. Even after they donned new gloves and the keys were cleaned, doubt ate away in the back of her mind.

When Kate stepped into the garage and Jake pulled up the steel door, light flooded in to reveal a baby blue 1955 Chevrolet Bel Air Nomad.

Chapter 5

The haul of food from Metro Grocery Store brought a lot of smiles to everyone on the island. Now that Grindstone was home base, it didn't take long for everyone to fall into a routine. It seemed almost ironic that the very man that had traumatized them was now dead and his property had become a haven for those in need of shelter.

It was established early on that no one person would be in charge. Any and all disputes that arose would be discussed weekly down at the local community hall. Any decisions that needed to be made required a majority vote.

In the time since moving over to the island, it had worked. Everyone assisted with the daily task of living and no one went without. Food was shared, clothing, tools, and everyone did their best to get along. Frank figured it wouldn't always be that way. People were people at the end of the day. The need for independence, the need to disagree was inherent in all. That's why he'd considered rebuilding his home on his island.

Frank gazed down at the burnt rubble, and sighed. What little remained was charred beyond comprehension. He fished through the charcoaled mess and retrieved the photo frame he'd been looking for. It was a photo of Kate, Ella and him in better days, back when Ella was only eight years of age. Now all that was left was a corner.

"We can help you rebuild."

Frank turned to find Landon Forester. It had been strange to see his doctor execute several of Guthrie's family. Then again, he'd had a hard time killing.

"Oh, hey doc."

"Manage to salvage anything?"

"A few metal tools that were in the basement, but the rest is a write off."

He nodded, trudging through the ash and cinder.

"So, I've been speaking with a few of the others about how we move forward."

Frank tossed him a confused look. "We are moving forward."

"No, I know. I just mean that we should consider looking at new ways of protecting the island. All the shifts of patrolling at night are beginning to exhaust folks. It's not good to be up through the night."

"We don't have much choice," Frank said, picking his way through some more of the debris.

"Of course we do. Some have considered erecting fencing. As much as I think that might have been doable back when society was functioning, it's too much work. So, some of us are considering moving back into Clayton."

Frank jerked around in shock. "You want to risk heading over to the mainland?"

"Well, at some point we have to start again, Frank. We can't live on this island."

"Why not?"

"It's not good for anyone."

"You mean it's not good for you?"

Landon smiled. "I enjoyed visiting our place but my wife wants to return to her home in Clayton. What am I supposed to tell her? That she can't?"

"Look, I don't care what people do, but I know that we are stronger together and after what we went through with the Guthrie's, I don't expect they will be the last group we'll knock heads with."

"Are you sure that isn't your paranoia kicking in, Frank?"

He grit his teeth. "I don't have paranoia."

"Fear. Paranoia. It's kind of the same, don't you think? Anyway, how are things with you?"

Landon wiped off some dirt from a foundational stone and took a seat. He got the same look on his face that he did every time Frank visited him for meds. The concept that what Frank had been suffering from could be cured was ludicrous to Landon. No, as long as they could push more pharmaceutical drugs, that was all that mattered, at least, that's what Frank thought.

"Well I'm not popping anxiety meds like candy if

that's what you're asking."

He nodded, his lip curling up. "That's good. Sal said you had been improving."

There was a pause between them. It was awkward. He'd never really got to know his doctor beyond seeing him for updates. He always was standoffish, professional, just the way Frank liked it. He didn't like getting too close to people, it meant they might force their way into his life, kind of like the way Sal had. Though Sal would never see it that way.

"You must want to get back home, Frank. I mean, it can't be easy staying in the house of the man you killed."

"I don't lose much sleep over it," Frank muttered, continuing the search for personal belongings. "Anyway, what is your incessant need to want to get off the island? I thought you liked the fact that everyone was chipping in with the work load?"

"I do, but like I said, Sandra wants a little more space."

"Space? The island is big enough for all of us." Then Frank clued in. His brow tightened. "You don't want to carry the load, do you?" He stared at Landon and Landon's eyes dropped. "You think it's below you because you were a doctor before all of this. Fancy house. Fancy car. Nice salary. And now you're one of us, just another guy stripped of what he has."

"Alright. Yeah, that's it. But you know what, I worked my ass off to become a doctor and I earned the right to be in a different pay grade from others."

Frank chuckled.

"What?" Landon asked.

"Listen to yourself. Life isn't going back to normal, Landon. If anything, it's just going to get worse."

"It doesn't have to."

"Maybe not, but what you had before this is gone. That's a fact." Frank dropped a piece of charred wood on the ground. "If this outbreak has taught me anything, it's that life can change on us real fast whether we are prepared or not. Rich or poor, the playing field has been leveled. So, if you want to know how we move forward from here, we move forward together, not apart. Hell, assholes playing around with viruses, trying to conquer and divide, it's the very thing that has got us into this mess. Do you know there was a time when humanity worked together? Communities helped each other and made sure that no one went without. Where people didn't lock themselves away in houses, hide behind computers or call, texting — communicating. I hate to say it, but perhaps this virus was the best thing that could have happened to us. At least now we have to rely on each other."

"So you don't agree. Is that what you're saying?"

Frank shook his head in disbelief. "You didn't hear a word of what I said, did you?"

"Of course I did, it just doesn't sit well with me."

"Oh for fuck sake, Landon, do you think any of this," Frank waved his arms around, "sits well with me?"

He spluttered. "Well... no... I just..."

"If you want to head over to Clayton, be my guest. I don't expect anyone is going to hold you back or deny you that right. But I would urge you to think this through. All we have is each other now. And to be honest. I don't think that's a bad thing."

With that said, Frank turned and strolled back down to his docked boat.

* * *

Chester gathered them all together to discuss the journey north. He couldn't take them all, as some would need to stay at the cottage and protect what little they did have, but in his mind, this was one trip that was going to be worth it. They sat on small logs around the afternoon fire. Smoke wiggled its way up into the air, taking with it glowing embers. A few of them coughed and sipped on beer. Pat was milking his shot foot for all it was worth. Since making his way back, Martha had been tending to him like a mother. At any minute now, he expected her to whip out one of her breasts and feed him. It was sickening the way he acted. The guy was a grown man and yet he was acting like he'd dodged death itself. Served him right. Fool.

"Listen up. As you are aware, our resources are low."

"I don't consider six months low," Tex piped up.

"Well, at the rate you are downing those beers, we are looking at needing to find more in the next week." Chester glared at him and pulled at his own collar that was beginning to feel a little tight. Even though he carried a fair amount of weight among them, not all of them hung on his every word. He hated the fact that he was going to have to sell them on this.

"I'm going to take Bobby, Sawyer, Tex, and Roy with me to Clayton, New York. It's only an hour away. We expect to be there a couple of days maximum, then we'll return.

"What about me?" Pat groaned.

Chester shook his head. "Well, you're the lucky one. You get to babysit Martha, the baby, Beatrix, and Sheila with James." He then gazed around and frowned. "Where is Beatrix, by the way?"

"Still out hunting."

Chester slapped his forehead hard. "Are you telling me no one has seen her since she went out?"

They all looked at each other dumbfounded. Tex was the first one up, rushing into the forest calling out to her. The rest of them, barring Pat and Martha followed suit. They spread out, calling her name and heading in the direction she was last seen earlier that day.

"Beatrix."

Chester ground his teeth. There was always one of them fucking everything up. Why on earth had he agreed to let them stay at his cottage? He thought, as he pushed through the thick brush calling her name.

It wasn't but ten minutes later that a gunshot was fired at them from above. All of them scrambled for cover and laughter erupted. Sitting in a tree seat, high up and completely camouflaged, was Beatrix, grinning from ear to ear. She was mental. Utterly out of her mind.

"What the hell are you playing at?" Tex shouted.

"There you go, Chester. I could have taken every single one of you out and you wouldn't have known. I told you I could do it."

"Get the hell down here," he demanded. This was all a

game to her. Twenty-six years of age and she had the intelligence of a five-year-old. He told her a week ago that she wasn't going to be involved in any of the runs or hunting because she was a woman and quite frankly, in his mind, they couldn't do shit except cook, clean and fuck. Of course, Beatrix saw red and wagged her finger in his face with all the hostility of an angry feminist. She told him she would prove him wrong, and that if he didn't watch his back, that perhaps he would end up with a bullet in his head. Sure enough, she meant it.

They watched as she slipped down the tree with all the finesse of a chimpanzee. Tex immediately jumped to the defense of his wife seeing that Chester was about to slap her up the side of the head.

"Now, now, Chester. She didn't mean anything by it."

"Yes I did, get the hell out of my way," Beatrix said trying to push past him.

"I'm warning you, Tex, keep her on a leash or else."

"Or else what? Uh? What are you going to do?"

Chester lunged forward and Tex knocked him back. "I

don't want to fight you, Chester, but she's my wife and I won't put up with it."

"Perhaps you should stay here," he muttered. "I'll take James."

Tex threw up his arms in protest. "Come on, Chester. I didn't mean it like that."

Chester sneered at him and trudged back to camp feeling humiliated. The others looked on as he passed them and he could feel their eyes boring into his back. He was losing control and he knew it. There were few among them that were willing to stand up to him besides Tex and his wife. It wasn't that he thought the rest were cowards, but they had more respect for his badge. Perhaps that's what he needed to wear. Something changed when he put that uniform on. People no longer saw him when he slipped into that crisp shirt; all they saw was an officer. Officers got respect. And right about now he could use a little of that.

Chapter 6

Misty Guthrie stood at the edge of the marina on the Canadian side, cursing under her breath. A harsh wind blew in, nipping at her ears. Bret was a coward. Just like Butch had said. So were the other women, except for Rachel. They'd been friends since school. If one of them was going down, so would the other. She sneered thinking of all the ways she was going to make them pay for they had done to Butch and the others. If Bret weren't going to do anything about it, she would. She peered through the binoculars again to get a better look.

"Do you see them?" Rachel asked.

"Oh yeah, yukking it up in our home, eating our food."

"Bastards."

She nodded. "Butch would turn in his grave if he could see this now."

She knew it wasn't going to be easy, but Misty wasn't

one for backing away. Bret had groveled before them. Pleaded with them to let them go. Sure enough, he got his wish, even though it was humiliating. Misty went along with it until they made it back to the mainland. Her thoughts drifted back to that moment.

"Enough Misty!" Bret shouted while gripping her arm tight. "What is done is done."

"You're a coward. They have just taken the entire island and you want to run away with your tail between your legs."

"It wasn't right what Butch did. He pushed them into a corner, how did you expect them to react? No, we are lucky they agreed to our terms. I say we move on to Maine. Get as far away from this place and perhaps we can carve out some smidgen of an existence."

"That's what a coward would say."

"I don't give a fuck what you think. You want to stay here, fine, but I am moving on. I should have gone to Maine when this all kicked off."

"Yeah, maybe you should have."

Though she didn't want to plead with him, she knew that

their chances were better in numbers.

"Look, okay, you are right," she said, trying to use some reverse psychology. "We should go, move on to Maine, but before we leave we are going to need some supplies for the journey."

Bret leveled up to her and she knew he wasn't buying it.

"You think I'm stupid? That might have swung with Butch, but not me. We leave now before they change their mind and kill the whole damn lot of us. We have children to think about here."

"Exactly. They sent children away. Children."

"And we shot one of theirs."

There was silence for a second.

"They got what they deserved for killing our kin."

"Our kin got what it deserved for stealing from them. No matter how you try to twist this and reason it out, Misty, you know as well as I do what Butch did was wrong."

"And so you are just going to be a pussy?"

She could see that he wanted to hit her. "Go on. Do it. I dare you." She enjoyed getting in his face and pushing his buttons. If Butch had been still there he would have put Bret on his ass by now. In her mind nothing had changed, she didn't take shit from him then, and she sure as hell wasn't going to take it now.

Bret lifted his hand, waving his finger near her nose. "We are done."

He turned with a few of the others. Some of the women looked forlorn as they gazed back over their shoulders gripping their children's hands. Misty grit her teeth and then started shouting.

"Go on, then. Go. We don't need you. You'd only get us killed anyway."

Bret turned around and gave her the bird. She contemplated for a moment putting a round in the back of his skull. She gripped at the rifle and lifted it but Rachel pushed it down.

"Let them go. It's not worth it."

She nodded, pursing her lips for a second. "Yeah, you're not worth it. You'll be dead before you make it to Maine."

She snapped back into the present moment and turned

towards Rachel, who was puffing on a cigarette.

"So, what now?"

She walked over to her and took the cigarette from the corner of her lips and placed it in her own mouth and took a deep inhale. It glowed a deep orange. "We bide our time. Observe them from a distance and look for opportunities to pick them off, one at a time."

"You don't want to go over there?"

"Hell no, look at how that worked out for Butch?"

"No, we'll let them come to us. We'll head back to Clayton and gather together a few more supplies from the store's basement. We'll stay there, perhaps even pay their homes a little visit." She got this devilish grin on her face. The thought of destroying their homes would at least let her blow off a little bit of steam. Butch would have liked it. He would have wanted them to strip them of all they had and make them suffer. And they would suffer. "It won't be long before they send out others on a run and we'll be waiting. Right now, we have the advantage. They think they're safe. They are far from safe."

She blew out gray smoke and her lip curled.

Chapter 7

The long journey would take them via Interstate 85 and then north on 81. A task that would test the patience of anyone on a good day — this wasn't a good day. They had stopped at a gas station somewhere between Charlotte and Blacksburg. Jake had gone into the store to see if anyone was around while Kate was in the vehicle. They hadn't been there more than a few minutes when two men wearing bandannas over their faces came out of nowhere and stuck a gun in her face and told her to get out of the vehicle. Meanwhile, Jake was completely oblivious to it all. Kate was in no position to fight and even the slightest hesitation was met with aggression. She was struggling to get out of the car because of her arm when the guy just yanked her to the ground. By the time Jake noticed, it was too late. They hopped in and tore away, leaving her groaning and soaked in a dirty puddle.

That was an hour ago.

Since then they had been trudging along the hard shoulder. Jake walked backwards sticking out his thumb. Like that was going to work. Picking up hikers was a no-no at the best of times, but now there was less chance of it.

"Why are you doing this?" Kate asked.

"Other than the fact that you are mortally wounded?"

"Mortally," she let out a chuckle then groaned from the pain in shoulder.

"Look, I need to know that my family is okay, and we'll be passing right through Pennsylvania."

"Right, if we make it that far. My feet are killing me."

He frowned. "Yeah, we need to find some transportation."

The cycle of trucks and cars shooting past them lasted for the better part of two hours. When they eventually made it to the nearest truck stop, which was just off Harmony road in North Carolina, they were famished, exhausted. It was dark, but they had passed a sign indicating a Fast Track rest stop just a few miles back.

"Burger Barn. Oh my God, could I do with a burger right about now."

"Yeah, best of luck with that."

They had been rationing out several granola bars, two bottles of water and some wine gums since Atlanta. Both of their stomachs were grumbling and irritation had begun to set in. Kate figured at the bare minimum if they couldn't find a vehicle, they could at least find a place to sleep for the night. The truck stop's close proximity to I-77 meant they could be back on track first thing in the morning. Though they had suffered some setbacks, they had every intention of reaching Clayton.

As the two of them made their way up 901, on their right was a small BP gas station, across the road was a Burger Barn, up from that a community bank, and farther down was the large truck stop with a 7-Eleven.

They could see trucks up ahead; some of them had light emanating from inside. A wave of relief rolled over them at the thought of finding someone who might be heading north. Being optimistic about the future was all they had left.

As they were getting closer to the main truck stop, Jake noticed another gas station further down called Union Grove Quick Stop.

"You think they might still have gas?"

"It's possible. Not every gas station would have stayed open until they were out. Though I highly doubt they do. Gas delivery would have stopped, the tanks below ground would likely be empty."

To the left and right of them in the large parking lots were different vehicles. Some of them were empty, one had its door open and a large dark mass was on the ground. Jake shone his flashlight on it and they diverted their gaze. It was blood.

They were about ten feet from the main entrance when the sound of gunfire erupted. It echoed and appeared to be coming from inside.

"Stay close," Jake said as they double-timed it over to the wall and tried to find cover in the shadows. A small amount of light came from flashlights beyond the windows. The truck stop was just an Esso station with a 7-Eleven attached. There was a small Subway restaurant off to the right of that.

They crept along the side to get a better view of what was happening. As they drew near they could hear voices. Jake was just about to take look when someone opened a door on a truck and jumped out. A heavy set man with a gut hanging over his belt snorted hard and then spat a wad of phlegm on the ground before lighting up a cigarette and doing up his zipper.

"Come on, get out," he said, turning back to his cab and holding the door open. A young woman, who couldn't have been more than mid-twenties, jumped out. Though the light from the cab was dim, she could tell the woman looked scared. She did up her top and he shoved her forward towards the Subway store. Every few feet he would grab her ass and the woman would flinch and try to escape his grasp.

No words were exchanged between the two of them. Jake and Kate pressed their backs to the wall and pulled back behind a corner to stay out of sight.

"Go on inside," the man said.

"Please just let us go."

Five words, but it would change the course of their journey, at least for Kate.

As soon as they heard the door swing closed, Jake was up. He grabbed a hold of her hand and they sprinted over to the truck. All the while, Kate was thinking of who that woman was. Jake pried open the truck door and forced his gun inside, just in case someone was still in there.

"Kate, the keys are in the ignition. Come on, let's go."

She shook her head. "Jake, I don't feel good about this."

"I'm not one for stealing shit, but someone did it to us. It's just the way this new world works."

"No, I don't mean that."

"Then what?"

Kate turned back to the store. "Did you hear that woman?"

He shrugged. "Who knows? Who cares! Let's get out

of here."

She nodded, and was about to go around when Jake raced over to a second vehicle and tried to start the engine. It didn't start. "Shit! Come on."

He tried again but it didn't even let out a splutter.

"Look, I might be able to hot wire this but I would need a few minutes. Hold this." Jake handed her the Glock. He then dropped down below the steering column with his small flashlight in his mouth and tore off the plastic below.

"I just need to disconnect the wires from the ignition system, strip the two red wires and twist them together."

He began fiddling with a Swiss Army knife that he had on a keychain and went about trying to get it rigged up. Kate had to know what was going on. Call it curiosity. A women's intuition, but nothing about what she heard felt right.

"Do you think you can hold the flashlight?"

Those were the last words she heard as she headed off in the direction of the Subway. She held the gun in her left hand and did her best to remain out of sight. When she reached the window, she was in a crouched position. She looked back at the truck and Jake had jumped down and was calling out to her but she just ignored him. From inside, she could hear two women crying.

"Shut up. Or I'll give you something to cry about."

That only made them cry harder. Circling her way around the back of the store, she noted that the back door was open. Someone had propped a few bricks against it. A brown sedan car was parked close by with the trunk open. As she approached, she heard a voice, so she ducked behind one of the large dumpsters. The smell was atrocious. It was bad in the summer heat but this stuff had to have been sitting here for months. Peering around the steel structure, she saw a different guy with a mustache come out the back holding a box. He dumped it in the trunk and went back in. Wasting no time, she rushed over to see what it was. Inside the box were cans of tomato, along with bread. Under the small dome light she could tell it had expired because the bread had turned a moldy green and yet they were still taking it. Desperate times meant people couldn't be picky.

Right then she felt a hand. She spun around to find Jake.

"What are you doing?" he said before casting a nervous glance inside the store.

"You're hungry right?"

He nodded but flashed a confused expression.

"I don't know what the situation is with the women, perhaps they are just family and being treated poorly, but I know I'm not leaving here without something to eat."

"Well, take the box and let's go."

"You grab it, it's too heavy."

The moment he did, she backed up and darted inside the store.

"Kate!" he said in a faint voice. In the darkness of the corridor, she pressed on towards the sound of voices. It smelled atrocious inside. Like death and rotten meat. That's when she saw where the smell was coming from. As she passed the kitchen, inside there was a mound of bodies. She squinted into the darkness, unable to believe what she was seeing. There had to have been more than twenty. They were piled up over each other haphazardly, just a sprawl of arms and legs and decaying flesh.

"You got all of it?"

"Yeah, we'll haul this over to the truck and get moving."

The sweet smell of tobacco drifted up the corridor. Kate brought up the gun and started heading in the direction when the same guy who had carried out the last box came into view. He was looking down in the box for a second, then he gazed up to see the barrel of the gun. His eyes widened and in that split second, two things happened: One, he threw the box at Kate, and she fired. The round missed and the mustached man ducked out of view. By now Jake had caught up with her just as the chaos erupted.

Kate pulled around the corner, keeping the gun out and her eyes darted around the Subway restaurant.

"Come out," she said. "There are more of us."

A pair of hands shot up and she directed her weapon in the direction of the skinny, mustached man. She couldn't tell what color hair he had or whether he had a weapon on him. Right then, a gun went off to her right. A flash of light and the round hit the wall. Kate was pulled back by Jake, who immediately took the gun from her.

"That's a dumb move, lady. If there is more of you, where are they?"

"Right here," Jake shouted.

"Two of you? And the rest?"

"Outside," he replied. "So be my guest, try and make a run for that truck and see how far you get."

Silence fell over them as they waited for the men to respond. They could hear them whispering and shuffling across the ground. No one had the advantage because it was pitch dark inside. All that was visible was the outline of the counter, tables, chairs and… A figure rose up and fired two more rounds, then they heard the sound of a bell, and the door opened. Jake returned fire, this time the window on the door smashed. But they were already hightailing across the park, turning only occasionally to fire back a few rounds. Glass shattered, smothering the floor in jagged shards.

"Anyone else still in there?"

A cry was heard. "Over here. They're gone."

Jake slipped inside the restaurant area with Kate close behind. Kate's eyes glossed over the trays of expired food that would have once been served. A decaying body lay draped over the counter still wearing a Subway uniform. Once they made their way around to where the tables were, they found two women huddled beneath one.

"It's okay, you can come out."

They were reluctant but slowly eased themselves out from their small enclosure. Kate stayed ten feet back from them. They were both frail looking, almost looked like junkies. Their clothes practically hung from their shoulders. Bony, sunken in eyes, and they smelled bad. Jake shone the light on them to check for infection. While they weren't in good shape, they certainly didn't look infected — yet. Jake went over to the main door to check that the men had gone. They hadn't taken the truck, which meant they were still in the area.

"Where are you two from?" one of the women asked.

It immediately threw Kate off. She expected them to plead or ask to be taken with them, or attempt to hug them for helping them escape those two lunatics.

"Atlanta."

"You have a vehicle? Food?"

"No."

Kate immediately turned the tables and began questioning them.

"Who were those men?"

"Oh, them." The one girl put her hands in her back pockets and cast a glance over her shoulder. "You shouldn't have done that," the other woman said.

"Why not, they were hurting you right?"

"Hurting?"

The two women looked at each other and Kate caught something. Her gut told her something was not right.

"Yeah, he had you in that truck, was shoving you and you said 'just let us go'."

A smirk danced on the shorthaired girl's lips. Before Kate could take another step back, one of them lunged at Kate with a knife. She sliced her arm. Kate let out a scream and Jake turned. The women rushed Kate and brought her down. Jake fired a round and struck one of them in the back. She collapsed but not before the other one put a knife to Kate's throat.

"Put the gun down. I'll cut this bitch right now."

Jake moved towards her slowly and Kate put her hands up. "Just do it, Jake."

"Put the weapon down," she yelled. The other woman who'd been shot was lying motionless, blood pooled around her body. The knife-wielding maniac pressed harder against Kate's throat and she was sure she would slash it.

"Put it down."

"Okay, okay. Just don't do anything."

Jake's movements were slow and purposeful. He

placed the gun on the counter. As he released his hand, she waved the knife in an outward motion telling him to get on the floor face down. Kate knew it was now or never. She reached up and grabbed her arm. They rocked back and forth on the ground wrestling for control.

It was the sound of a gun going off, and the woman's body going limp behind her that caused Kate to relax. Ahead, Jake stood holding his Glock, his hands trembling.

Chapter 8

Landon Forrester was a stubborn man liable to cause a tear among the survivors. Frank stood with the others as his family hugged it out before leaving for the mainland. Something Frank had noticed in every facet of life was when one people moved home, changed careers or chose to distance themselves from an organization, it created waves. Though the ones left behind would say they were happy, inside it raised questions. Should I stay? Why am I being left behind? Do I value what I have or should I be looking for something new? Everyone perceived life as being better on the other side of the fence, when in reality, it rarely was. It was just more bullshit repackaged and served up by different assholes.

He wasn't here to babysit them. If they honestly thought they could survive without them, then it was on their heads. Still, the rest of the survivors had agreed at a town hall meeting that they would check in on them a few times a week to make sure.

What they really meant was, they would check to see if it was working and if so, they would follow suit. People were odd. They didn't know a good thing when it was in front of them. He could already tell by the conversation Landon had with the group that others would follow. Frank understood the desire for space, privacy and independence, but what they had on Grindstone Island wasn't taking that away. In many ways, it was adding to it. On the island, if there was a problem they could address it fast, but being off the island, it just meant delays.

Landon reached Frank and extended his hand. "Thanks again, Frank. I appreciate what you had to say and I hope you won't take this as me snubbing you, but I have to do what is right for my family."

"We can't protect you off the island. You know that, right?"

He nodded. "It's my job to protect my family. No one else."

Frank squeezed his hand tight and he made his way down to a boat. The rest of the families waved and acted as though they were just returning to a normal world. But this wasn't normal. It was far from it. Frank couldn't help thinking that it was a death sentence. But no one could prevent people from leaving. He'd made it clear right from the get-go that the only way life on the island would work is if they worked together. If anyone chose to disagree they could either discuss it or leave. No one would be forced into doing anything they didn't want to do. The only thing that wouldn't be tolerated was laziness. So far, they hadn't seen anyone not willing to chip in — except for Landon. The guy thought he was above the others because he was a doctor. Titles didn't mean anything now.

"You think he will be okay?" Ella asked, cupping a hand over his eyes to block the glare of a hard morning sun.

"If he isn't, he brought it upon himself."

Frank turned to head back to the house. Ella caught

up with him. "It's his right to do what's best for his family."

"Of course it is, but we are all part of a larger family now, and our individual decisions don't just affect one group within that, they affect us all. By leaving he has not only made his family vulnerable to attack, but he's weakened this island and made it that much more difficult for us. Now we'll have to travel across to the town when someone gets sick. No doubt he will expect us to book in with him." He scoffed. "Is his wife going to be his receptionist? The guy is deluded. He thinks that the world is going back to the way it is — it's not!"

"Then why are you attempting to rebuild the house on our island?"

"What?"

"If life is only going to get worse, then why are you going through all the trouble to try and establish what is gone?"

Frank slowed his pace and looked off across the St. Lawrence river. Maybe he wasn't that different than

Landon. Learning to accept that the world that they lived in had changed was a tough pill to swallow.

"That island. That home meant a lot to your grandparents, to me and to your mother."

"That island is isolation. It's the past, Dad," Ella said. "Like mom. When are you going to stop clinging to the past?"

"The day I die."

With that, he trudged off towards the house.

* * *

Landon took a deep breath, feeling like a weight had been lifted off his shoulders. He glanced back at his wife and kids and relished the thought of returning to their home and establishing some sense of normality. It wasn't that he disagreed with Frank. What he said made sense, but at what point did society get up, brush itself off and try to rebuild again? Those on the island were content with the status quo. They liked the security and democracy that had been established. Sure, he appreciated being able to sleep at night without the thought of getting his throat cut, but it wasn't the nights that made life. It was the daylight hours in between and he was tired of doing menial tasks, tasks that he would have paid people to do before the pandemic.

"Do you think

we are going to have enough food to eat, Landon?"

"Oh yeah, don't worry about it."

What he hadn't told Frank was that it was actually his idea to leave, not Sandra's. If she had her way, she would have stayed. It was okay for her. All she had to do was look after the kids and help out around the island once in a while, but him, no, he couldn't keep doing that. At first he thought he could. That was then, this was now. He didn't work his ass off through med school to live out the rest of his life taking orders from folks who worked at the local 7-Eleven.

The boat kicked up over a choppy wave and he felt fear flood through him. It was the unexpected that was worrying, not finding food. He didn't have a problem scavenging for food and at least this way, he wouldn't have to share it. They might actually eat better. The whole rationing thing was starting to wear him down. But, if he was honest, it was protecting his family that concerned him the most. But that was a risk he was willing to take. That risk existed before the downfall of society. Home invasions, attempted murder, attacks on people might not have been as common as they were now, but they existed. That's what he told himself as they got closer to Steel Point Marina on the East side of Clayton.

He brought the boat into the dock and tried to remain optimistic. He'd spent the better part of a month trying to convince her it was best for them. Being holed up on some island wasn't any way to live. Besides, after two months he'd imagined the folks over in Clayton, the ones who had survived, would be trying to pick up the pieces, right?

The absence of people at the dock wasn't a good sign. Landon hopped out and tied it off. He was concerned about someone stealing the boat, but what could he do?

He didn't have any alternative until he could find a trailer, a truck and gas — if any existed.

After helping his family out, they made the short trek towards their home on Riverside Drive. It was a five minute walk at best. He lugged what little belongings they had down the road with his family trying to keep up. What a difference two months had made. He hadn't been back since leaving. Perfectly cut lawn grass was overgrown, bushes that would have usually been cut back by neighbors were wild and unkempt, flowerbeds were overloaded with weeds, and several homes had been destroyed by fire.

As they strolled up to the white, double car garage with an American flag blowing in the gentle breeze, he felt hope rise. He turned back to his family, beaming.

"Look kids, we're home. I'm telling you. I have a good feeling about this."

And in that moment he did.

"I want to check the mail," his youngest daughter Shelly said. She rushed up and pried it open and frowned.

Of course there was nothing inside, but Landon didn't care. They were home.

From the house, they had a beautiful view of the river, and once he had located a good pair of binoculars he could keep an eye on the island from this side. In his mind, it was perfect. Why have everyone on the same island when a few families could live in Clayton and keep their eyes open for any threats approaching the island.

"I don't know about this, Landon." Sandra looked around cautiously at the surrounding homes. No one was out but then why would they be? He assumed they would either be inside locked up tight or in town trying to clean up the streets. He gave her a reassuring hug as they made their way up to the house.

* * *

The men at the truck stop never returned. Well, perhaps they did, but Kate and Jake didn't stick around to find out. Tired, hungry and unsure of how many others were out there, they chose not to linger. Jake hotwired a car they found in an abandoned lot across from the truck stop. It was a crapped out Ford sedan that could have been featured on a unaired episode of Pimp My Ride. On the outside it just looked like a typical black four door Ford Falcon from the 90s, but inside they had it all blinged out with colorful accessories.

"Couldn't you have found a vehicle that didn't look like Joseph's Technicolor Dreamcoat?

"At least the radio works."

"Oh yeah, we can listen to white noise all the way home," Kate muttered, throwing him a smile.

Before leaving they had entered the Ace hardware store. Its windows had been smashed in and someone had dragged out some of the garden furniture products, as they were strewn all across the parking lot. They had high hopes of finding a knife or a hammer, something that Kate could use to protect themselves beyond the gun they had. The aisles were covered in all manner of tools. Shelving units had been pushed over and in the darkness of the previous evening all they had managed to find was a long pair of needle nose pliers and a screwdriver. It was crazy to think that people would have looted this place in the hope that the world would return to normal. Jake took what he could find and loaded it into a tool belt and handed it to Kate.

"Great, I should be able to hold off the masses with this," she said sarcastically. "I feel like Tim the Toolman Taylor."

"At least you might be able to fix that heap of crap out there if it breaks down."

By the time the afternoon arrived the following day they had made good progress. They had arrived in Morgan Town, located in West Virginia, over six hours away. They had slept in the vehicle overnight at a rest stop. Kate didn't get much sleep. She kept hearing noises and seeing the faces of those women back at the truck stop. She was paranoid that the men were going to follow them. But the truth was that not everyone wanted to die. People were opportunists. They would sweep in and steal if it didn't mean getting shot. It was the insane ones that worried her. They were out there, of that she was sure.

Those two women were proof of that.

Despite the fact that the car looked like it was on its last legs, they were able to get far on a tank full of gas,

siphoned from several of the vehicles in the vicinity. A task that caused Jake to throw up as he ended up swallowing a little gas as he sucked it out of the tank into a bucket. Though Kate wanted to just keep going, Jake's back was killing him because the bucket seats were covered in hard leather that didn't conform too well.

"We need to eat. I'm starving."

In their hurry to leave they hadn't eaten, and both of them were running on empty. Jake had a killer headache coming on and she was feeling nauseated. They followed the signs for the nearest mall and headed in that direction.

As they pulled into the parking lot, it didn't resemble the one they had come from. RVs were parked in various places and people were milling around. People didn't appear to be fighting. It was though they had established the parking lot as a sanctuary. Kate saw a Red Cross truck, and several workers handing out blankets. Jake smiled and they both breathed a sigh of relief as the vehicle spluttered upon entering the car park. Jake brought the window down as he pulled up alongside an RV. A young family were sitting on camping chairs around a small table eating lunch.

"Is there a place to get something to eat here?"

"Red Cross over there. Military are on site."

Kate leaned over Jake's lap. "And medical supplies?"

"They have them, but you will need to get checked out if you are thinking of staying. You a local?"

"From out of town. Atlanta."

"That's a long way. How's it down there?"

"Bad. Really bad."

The man got up but kept his distance from the vehicle. "I'm Wyatt by the way."

"Kate. Jake." They both said at the same time.

"Just follow that truck," he pointed towards a white one that had just pulled in. "They have a system here. It's not ideal but better than starving to death."

Kate nodded and thanked them before they went on

their way. For the first time since the pandemic had kicked off, Kate felt a smidgen of hope. It was good to see that not everyone was turning on each other.

A military jeep shot by them, followed by a large truck. As soon as it pulled up, several guys hopped out with M4's in their hands and watched over it. No doubt it had more supplies. They weren't taken chances and rightfully so. How many other cities were like this? And if everyone worked together, how soon could they be back up and running? As Jake pulled into a parking spot, and she got out, the smell of food hit her nostrils and both of them looked at each other with glee.

"Perhaps you will get that burger after all."

Chapter 9

Chester stepped out of the cottage in full regalia. His uniform was crisp and looked every bit the way it did when he set off for work in Lowville. That was exactly what he wanted. Nothing could be out of place. He puffed out his chest and donned his regular pair of aviator glasses before locking and loading a shot gun to get their attention. Their eyes widened as he adjusted his sidearm.

"Well, you maggots, are you ready to head out?"

He glared at them from behind his sunglasses and lit a cigarette. He blew the smoke out the side of his mouth. Roy was the first one up, followed by Bobby and Sawyer. Both James and Tex stepped forward; neither of them wanted to stay.

"Well, both of you aren't coming."

"You said I could go," James muttered.

"No, he said I could, he only mentioned your name because of..." Tex glanced at Beatrix. Chester snorted.

He already had in mind who was going but he thought he would have a little bit of fun with them before.

"Well, the way I see it, it looks like there is only one way to settle this. Power up the ATVs, you are going to duel it out."

"What?" both of them said in unison before looking at each other.

Chester walked over to the woodpile and dug out a large branch that hadn't been chopped up yet. He picked up a machete and began hacking way at the limbs.

"A joust, you idiots. You'll ride ATVs. One of you at one end, the other down that end. Whoever falls off first gets to stay behind." He continued chopping away until he had all the limbs off and a nice straight branch in his hand. He hacked off the excess and then handed it to Roy.

"Roy, wrap some cloth around that and use a bit of duct tape to secure it."

Roy smirked, finding it amusing. He stepped forward and went to work on it while Chester prepared the next.

Every now and then he would glance at them and chuckle.

"Of course, one of you can always stay here. Your decision."

Neither of them were giving an inch. It was pretty clear why. Sticking around the cottage would have meant more work. Fewer people, less sleep. And no one wanted to keep an eye on Beatrix. The girl was a handful. From the age of eight to twenty-one she had been a firecracker. A tomboy at heart, Tex found that appealing in some odd way and he married her by the time she was twenty-two. She'd grown up on a farm with a house full of boys. It was to be expected that she might be a little rough around the edges. In her case, she was just rough.

Ten minutes later they had them both set up at either end of the clearing decked out with jousting poles and rolls of blankets around their front and motorcycle helmets on. Neither one of them wanted to do it but they wouldn't back down. He decided to let them make fools of themselves. It would be his last moment of enjoyment before heading north to deal with Talbot.

Chester leaned back in a rocking chair in the middle of the porch like a king overseeing the match. Roy, Sawyer and the rest of them straddled logs, eager to see them go at it.

"Now just go easy," James said.

"This is going to be easy," Tex added before sliding down the visor on the motorcycle helmet. The ATVs let out a growl as they came to life. Both of them revved their engines waiting for Beatrix to drop the white cloth. Chester leaned forward in his chair and sipped at his beer with eager anticipation.

Beatrix waved the cloth around and then dropped it. Both ATVs shot forward kicking up dirt while Tex and James raised their poles and prepared to stab each other. Of course that wouldn't happen, unless they slipped and it got caught on their throats, as two bulletproof vests and blankets protected their torsos.

The first pass they both missed, the second time around they struck each other in the chest. James wobbled and it looked as if Tex was about to come off but he managed to hang on at the last second. Chester looked at the faces of the rest looking on. There was excitement. Roars of laughter erupted. Even Pat had stopped moaning about his foot and was cackling like a hyena. There was something very raw to what they had now. Perhaps it had gotten lost in the shuffle, in the need for humanity to evolve and grow beyond small communities that interacted with one another. This was the kind of fun that could only be had when risk was involved. It was probably why the Roman Empire tossed gladiators in the Coliseum and forced them to fight. This was how it would be from now on. Entertainment would no longer be found in front of a laptop, inside a cinema or one of the other mind-numbing activities that people spent all their goddamn time on. Folks would have to get creative.

On the third turn around, both of them revved their engines and unleashed everything they had at one another. Both leaned forward. Tex even stood up, taking both hands off the handles to ensure that he gave James one hell of a whack. Instead of plowing into him, he reared it back like a giant baseball bat and whacked him full force in the head. James flew off the back and landed hard. Everyone cheered and clapped as Beatrix rushed over to congratulate Tex on winning.

Chester smirked as he watched James get up and throw his helmet down in frustration. Tex came over with a smile spread across his face and his arm wrapped around Beatrix.

"Well, well, well... Good job, Tex."

He glanced over at James, who sneered.

"So when do we leave?" Tex asked.

Chester rose from the rocker and walked past him. "You don't."

"What? But I won."

"Well, technically you didn't because you stood up, but if it means so much to you, okay, you won. However, that doesn't change anything."

"I... I don't get it? You said if I won I would be

going."

"No, I said you both couldn't decide so you would need to duel it out."

His features screwed up and Chester could see that he was having difficulty understanding. "I already picked who was going."

"Who?" Tex demanded to know.

"Beatrix."

Beatrix's eyes widened. "What?"

Even James came running back, slack jawed and protesting. "That's not right, Chester."

"Of course it is. Beatrix has been on at me to let her hunt, so I'm giving her the opportunity."

Tex elbowed his way through and grabbed a hold of Chester. "Now listen here."

Chester turned sharply and brought his gun up under his jaw. "Do we have a problem?"

Tex tossed up his hands and swallowed hard. "No. Um. No."

"Don't you ever place your hands on an officer again.

This world might have gone to the shitter, but I am still to be shown some respect. You understand?"

Tex's hesitation caused Chester to press it harder against his head.

"Okay. Alright. I get it."

"Good. Beatrix, get your stuff together, you leave with us in ten minutes."

Beatrix glanced at Tex for a second before rushing into the cottage to grab a few things. She might have been his wife, but she was independent minded and certainly more capable than Tex. He'd noticed that the very moment Beatrix spoke up for herself. It wasn't just her creativity in luring them out to the forest that sealed the deal. It was her refusal to back down. He needed people like that. The fact that she was a female didn't matter. She had strength to her.

* * *

That evening Misty Guthrie watched in the shadows as Landon went about building a fire out the back of the house. It's what had caught her attention. She didn't see them arrive by boat, but when she and Rachel had been out scavenging for food, it was the smoke that drifted through the woods that caught her attention.

Now as they sat at the edge of a cluster of trees, she grinned.

"I told you they would come to us."

"What now?" Rachel asked.

"Time to play a game."

Rachel tossed her a confused look and she motioned for Rachel to follow. Crouching down, they scurried across the front of yard and peered in through the window. Several candles were lit inside. The flames flickered and shadows danced on the walls. Sandra was in the kitchen while the two kids were playing with toys.

"Right, here's what we are going to do," Misty said, pulling out a large bowie knife.

* * *

Landon poked at the flames. It crackled and popped and he squinted as smoke went in his eyes. With the small box of supplies the island group had given them before they left he figured they would have enough to last for at least five days before they would need to explore the town. He probably would go out sooner to avoid being in a position of panic. He cocked his head from side to side to work out the kinks. There was something very comforting to being back at his home. He turned and looked to see Sandra working away preparing supper in the kitchen. It wasn't ideal. In fact, he wished the electricity was on but he felt confident that they could make a go of it. He gazed out across the water and saw a few small fires. They weren't far away. If trouble arose and they really didn't think it was safe to stay, they could return. But without trying, how would they ever know when it was time to return to normal life?

Frank was wrong. This could work. It had to work. He couldn't keep living the way they had on the island, even if they were growing out their own food and had people patrolling around the clock.

Landon hadn't made it this far in his life to resort to relying on others. He didn't need anyone else except his family. That was it. It was easier this way. No disagreements. No arguments. No need to back down. They followed his lead.

How long would it take before Frank or one of the others would become like Butch? They had already come up with a few rules. That was the final nail in the coffin for Landon. He couldn't endure another town hall meeting. They made out as though everyone had a say, but that was just bullshit. How could anything be achieved that way? He'd tried, he really had, but watching everyone argue about the way they should go about surviving wasn't something he was ready to put up with.

He smiled as he tossed another thick log into the fire. He lifted his hands and warmed them and thought about what activities he could do with the children. Perhaps he would dig out the old fishing lines from the garage and take them down to the water. Sandra could bring a basket of food and they could have a picnic. There was a pandemic. So? It didn't mean they had to suffer.

That, of course, was the upside to a pandemic. There

was no one to treat because it was incurable, which meant he had more time on his hands to dedicate to Sandra and the children. She had always been going on about him spending more time away from his work. Well now—

"Landon! Landon!"

Her voice didn't sound panicked but there was an edge to it. He jogged up to the house and entered the back door.

"Are the kids with you?"

"No, I thought they were with you."

Panic washed over him as he rushed up stairs, calling out their names. "Shelly? Robin?" He made it to the top of the stairs and searched through the rooms, thinking that perhaps they were playing hide and seek. Though they were excited to get home and play with their familiar toys, they had been pleading with him for hours to have a game of hide and seek.

"Shelly, this is not funny. Come on out now."

He checked the closets, under the beds and in the bathroom but they were nowhere to be found. That's when something caught his eye. It was a flickering flame coming from the front of the house. He approached the window and saw someone standing outside looking up at the windows. They were wearing a balaclava mask and holding Shelly by her throat.

"Shelly!"

The figure dragged the girl away into the tree line. Utter terror filled his being as he bolted out of the room and shot down the stairs and out the front door. He darted across the green in the direction of the tree line with little thought to his own safety. He screamed out the names of his children and frantically searched the trees that surrounded his property.

He hadn't been out there for but a few minutes when he heard Sandra scream. Breathing hard and racing back as fast as he could, tears began to well up in his eyes. This had been a big mistake. He'd forced them to come over to the island. Promised them it would be safe. All because he couldn't endure doing menial work for others or handle the small amount of rationing.

When Landon burst through the front door, Sandra was gone. His eyes darted around the room.

"Sandra?"

Silence.

He repeated her name again. He reached for a lamp that was on the side and took the top off it. It was the first thing he could think to grab. Crossing the room, heading towards the kitchen, his pulse was beating rapidly and he could hear blood rushing in his ears.

"Sandra?"

A cry, like the sound of a dog whimpering, followed by another, terrified him.

I need the...gun. Shit! It's outside. Shit! He'd placed it down on the ground while he chopped up wood. Landon tossed the lamp. Driven to protect his family, he sprinted towards the back door, swung it open only to feel a hard thump in his stomach. His eyes dropped down to see an axe embedded in his torso, and still holding it was a figure wearing a balaclava. Blood rushed up into his mouth as he tried to tell them to leave his kids alone, but it only came out as a gurgled mess.

He collapsed to the ground and looked up to see the person unmask.

Misty Guthrie.

She loomed over him with a smile on her face. It would be the last face he would see.

Chapter 10

A bright sun bore down on them the next day. Frank had gathered together a crew of people to help. He took Gabriel, Zach, Tyrell and four of the other survivors over to his island to start work on clearing through the rubble. In some ways he was excited about it. It would make for a nice break from the routine of scavenging. The way he saw it, he had all the time in the world now on his hands. And one thing that society wouldn't be short on was lumber, stone and kitchen counters. He'd already started to sketch out a rough blueprint for the house. This time around he would use the finest lumber, the best granite tops and pack it with high-end utilities. In the event society was restored to its former self, this would be payment for all the shit he had to endure.

"I don't see the point of this," Tyrell muttered as he sifted through burnt fragments. "This is going to take us weeks to get this place cleared away and leveled out."

"It will if you keep dragging your ass," Gabriel said.

They were using shovels to fill up wheelbarrows and then two people were taking turns to take it down to the shore and dump it.

"There are perfectly good homes on Grindstone."

"Tyrell, did you father ever work on old cars?"

"No."

"Anyone you know restored a classic vintage car?"

"No."

"Okay, maybe you are the wrong person to talk to. Look, this place means a lot to me. It's been in our family for years, and well, if society returns to normal, we aren't going to be able to stay on Grindstone. Everyone will have to return home. So just as people prepare for the worst-case scenario, they must also be prepared for society to be restored."

"Okay. You have an apartment in Clayton. Just use that."

"Do you know how much it would cost to rebuild this house?"

Tyrell shook his head despondently.

"That's what insurance is for. Let them cover it."

"After the damage that has been done in the country, companies would be paying out of the nose for insurance. Half of it won't even be covered. I'm sure they would have some fine print that excludes them from viruses. Do you really think the insurance companies are going to return and deal with all those claims? No way. This pandemic has given every business in the world an excuse to disappear. Those who were about to suffer bankruptcy. Boom. Gone. Those who were holding millions of dollars of homeowners' money. Boom. Gone. Nope. Now is the time to take what we want. While the law isn't there to stop us."

"But that's theft," Zach muttered.

"Yeah, I'm not sure Ella would take kindly to that idea," Gabriel added.

"Then I guess they are going to have to lock us all up. What the hell have you all been doing since this kicked off? Scavenging. Taking. Stealing what was not yours."

Zach stopped working and wiped sweat from his face with the front of his t-shirt.

"Yeah, but that's different. The government would understand that. Hell, everyone has had to do that."

Tyrell started chuckling. "When did you grow a conscience? If anyone is going to get locked up it's you. Or have you forgotten about the solider you shot?"

Tyrell continued laughing but no one else did. Zach tossed his shovel down and trudged off.

"Good one, Tyrell," Gabriel said, shaking his head.

"What?" Tyrell tossed a hand up. "Oh, come on, Zach. You know I was joking."

There was an awkward silence between them all for a while before Frank continued.

"Anyway, I call it a fair trade. I take what I find as payment for them not having a better infrastructure in place to deal with this shit storm when it began."

Frank kicked at a chunk of wood until it broke apart, then scooped up some of the ash and tipped it into the barrel behind him.

Tyrell leaned on his shovel and took a long pull on his bottle of water. He wiped the sweat from his brow and gazed out across the water.

"You think Landon was right?"

"Oh don't you start. We're already expecting others to follow suit."

"Sure, but it's not like what he's saying doesn't make sense. It's been two months since the pandemic started. At what point do you go back to the way things were?"

"We don't, numbnuts. There is nothing left for it to be the way it was," Gabriel muttered.

"Of course there is. And anyway, are you telling me you are going to stay up here for the rest of your life? What about your family? Don't you want to find out if they are still alive? What about college?"

Zach returned a moment later with a bottle of water from a package they had brought over. He said nothing but just went back to working.

"College? That's fresh. Coming from the person who didn't give two shits about it and spent more time smoking a bong in his room and asking others for a copy of their work."

"Alright. I like to enjoy myself, but isn't that the whole point of college?"

Gabriel laughed out loud. "Yeah, I think that's what I saw on the application in fine print. An education is optional." Gabriel nudged Zach.

"No, you know what I mean. Anyway, it's a serious question. You guys might not agree with Landon, but I think he raises a valid point. All anyone talks about is surviving. Getting food and water and making sure we are safe, but what about starting again?"

"It doesn't matter," Frank said.

"But building your home does?"

"It's different."

"How?"

"This has sentimental value."

"And my life before this didn't?"

Frank stopped working and took a seat on an overturned bucket. He cracked open a can of soda and downed it before glancing up at Tyrell and addressing him.

"Okay, humor me. How do you suggest society rebuilds? Where do they begin?"

"Go back to work, clean up, sanitize, get the power grid back on. Look, we didn't suffer anything that knocked out America's infrastructure. Sure, there are buildings that might have to be knocked down and areas in cities and towns that will need to be cleared away, but not everything was ruined. "

"And how do you intend to convince everyone to come out of their burrows and get back to it?"

"Well…" he paused. "I don't know. Maybe the President can announce it."

"Yeah, I can hear it now," Gabriel said picking up his shovel and using it like a microphone.

"Attention Americans. This is your President. Listen up you lazy assholes. It's time to get back to work. We have suffered a great loss. Most of society is dead and clogging up the roads, we're not too sure how clean buildings are, so be sure to wear a pair of gloves. My recommendation is the 100% cotton ones being sold on the Shopping Channel. And if you… buy today, we'll throw in a clean jock strap."

Tyrell tossed a piece of wood at him.

"Why do I bother? You're—"

"Dad!"

Frank jerked his head to see Ella rushing up towards them. "You need to come quickly."

"What? What's going on?" He reached for his rifle that was perched against a tree, fully expecting to engage with a nearby enemy threat.

"It's Landon."

All of them abandoned what they were doing and joined Ella in the boat. She engaged the throttle and they took off over the choppy dark waters. Mist sprayed up their faces as she pushed the engine to its limits. Out of breath, she forced words out. "This morning Tom went over to discuss with Landon about his family moving back to Clayton as well. Their whole family has been slaughtered."

"What?" Frank grappled with the news. A shot of fear flooded his being.

A cold wind nipped at their ears and the sound of thunder only added to the sense of impending trouble. As soon as they arrived at the dock, Tom was there to meet them along with Mark Bolmer. Both of them looked disturbed.

"Where are they?"

"I'll take you to them. Be warned though, it's not a pretty sight," Mark said. Tom chose to hang back. He was looking green in the face and still wasn't coping well with what he witnessed.

As they made their way down to his house, Frank kept his rifle shouldered. Tyrell stayed back with Ella while Zach and Gabriel came along. They jogged the short distance. As they got closer, Frank's eyes widened.

Hanging from a large oak tree out in front of their home were the four bodies of the Forrester family. The only one that had a fatal wound was Landon. The others had their hands tied behind their backs and were hung. Frank raised his hand to the bridge of his nose and shook his head. The sight of those children hanging there was the hardest part to see.

"Any message left behind?"

"Nothing. I checked the house. It was in a mess. There was blood on the back porch which seems to indicate that's where they got Landon. But beyond that, nothing."

They took a few minutes to go through the home and look for anything that might indicate who might have done it. Had this been done randomly? It wouldn't have been a far stretch of the imagination to assume that others came by and scavenged their home and in the process killed them. Landon wasn't exactly a man for backing down. He probably fought back while the others were subdued.

"Cut 'em down. We'll bury them here on the property."

The next hour was spent digging graves for them. All the time, Frank felt on edge. He kept looking over his shoulder, wondering if the people who had done this were nearby and watching.

"You think we should check the surrounding houses?"

"For what?"

"Other survivors who might have seen it."

"We're not cops. It's not our job. From now on, no one comes over to Clayton unless they are armed and in a group of no less than four."

"Did anyone find Landon's weapon?"

"Highly doubt they left it," Zach said. Frank wrapped the bodies in white sheets from the house with Mark's help before placing them inside the earth. They covered it up and created a small mound, then created crosses to be inserted into the top. When they were done all of them were covered in dirt, sweat and grime.

"You think we should say a few words?"

"What? Like, I told you so?" Tyrell said before chuckling.

Frank grabbed a hold of him and threw him against a tree. "You think this is funny? Two kids murdered. You still think this is a game? That you can go back to living your old life?"

"Get off me, man."

"Frank," Gabriel tried to pry him away from Tyrell, but he was fuming. The guy had acted like the whole thing was just one big gag since the first day they had picked him up. There was something definitely wrong with his head.

"Asshole."

Frank let go and Tyrell stormed off in a huff. Mark said a prayer before they returned to the boat. Ella met him halfway and asked where Hayley was.

"What are you on about?" Gabriel said.

"I thought he would have told you," she said. "Mark came over with Hayley and Meghan. Frank turned to Mark, who was getting into the boat.

"Mark. Where's Hayley?"

His eyebrows shot up. "Shoot! When we arrived they said they were going into town."

"You have got to be kidding me. You let her go into

town?"

"She was with Meghan."

Frank turned around and started heading back up the road along with Gabriel and Zach.

"I'm coming with you."

"No, stay with the others."

"That's not happening. Not this time. I'm coming."

Ella shouted

to Tom, Mark, and Tyrell that they would be back in an hour.

As they trudged on towards the town of Clayton, Frank had a bad feeling about this.

Chapter 11

Leaving Morgantown was harder than she thought it would be. It wasn't exactly the city itself that held any appeal. It was like every other that had been decimated by the spread of the virus, but it was the infrastructure they had in place. So far, it was the closest they had seen to normal civilization. Military vetted everyone, placed them in quarantine if they chose to stay, but at no point was anyone treated like a prisoner. If they wished to leave, they could. They were even offered to be driven to a location just beyond the perimeter of the shopping center.

They didn't have much, but with the little they had, they were making it work.

It gave Kate hope to know that pockets of society were banding together to survive and not just simply hiding away hoping that someone was going to deal with the aftermath. The fact was, she knew first hand from countless meetings at the CDC that there was no one person conducting the survival of the nation. At least, that's what she was told. Perhaps from the safety of Mount Weather efforts were being made, but she doubted it. And if in the slim hope they did find a way to turn the tide, it would take forever to get a cure out to the masses.

It could be months, even years, before society was back on its feet.

Jake and Kate continued up I-68 north, cutting through Pennsylvania. The plan was to stop in on his family and check on their wellbeing.

Kate stared out at the numerous vehicles littering the highway. It had become a morgue of the dead. Bodies were in various states of decay.

"Crazy to think that no one has touched them."

"No one will. Would you?"

Jake threaded the vehicle around charred cars until they made it to the turn off. His family was located in a city called Williamsport. It butted up against the West Branch Susquehanna River.

"Have you ever been here before?"

"No," Kate replied.

His lip curled up. "It's the birthplace of Little League Baseball."

"You did it as a kid?"

"Who didn't?"

They turned down a street that cut through the downtown area. It was deserted.

Several stray dogs stood around a garbage can that was overturned, scavenging what they could from the moldy remains. Their heads turned as they drove past and they darted into some nearby bushes. Were they scared of being killed for food? It seemed an outlandish thought but who knew what lengths people would go to.

An old woman pushing a shopping cart packed with clothes and various camping items eyed them both before hurrying down the road. She almost lost her footing as she drove the cart with a wonky wheel down a curb. Several items dropped to the ground, and she scooped them up and continued on.

As they drew close to the neighborhood his family lived in, six men and several women darted out in front of their vehicle, causing Jake to slam the brakes on. They banged on the windows to be let in. It was hard to know if they were trying to hijack or eager to escape the suffering. Kate checked her door. Thankfully, the locks were engaged. Jake pounded the horn and it let out several honks.

"Don't open."

"Honestly, Jake, you must think I just stepped out of the looney bin. Their hands, faces and clothes were dirty and they looked as if they had been living it rough for several weeks.

Kate flashed the gun and didn't even have to say a word. They backed up and Jake peeled away from them. Kate glanced back in her rearview mirror. It was painful to see so many desperate and needy people, but it was the way things were now. They had to be careful. They had no clue who was infected. Then it dawned on her as she placed the gun back down.

"Those women back at the truck stop. You don't think?"

"If they were, we'll be spitting blood in about ten hours."

Stupid decisions were made in the heat of the moment. Everyone was prone to make mistakes. Though she knew better than to wander into a station with armed individuals, she truly had the women's best interests at heart. It would have eaten away at her if she had just walked on. And yet that's what they had to do now, wasn't it?

Everyone would view the end of the world differently. Some would see it as an opportunity to prove themselves, others would seek to help, most would avoid people and the rest, well, they didn't care.

It didn't take them long to reach Jake's parents' home.

"What about brothers and sisters?"

"I have none," he said, turning into the gravel driveway that led up to a home shrouded by trees. From the road it was hard to see the place, but once they turned the corner Kate was surprised to see a mansion. Of course he noticed that some of the homes looked better than the ones they saw closer to the downtown, but... her eyes widened.

"You're rich?"

He chuckled. "My father is fairly wealthy."

"Fairly?"

"It doesn't matter now. For all the money in the bank, he can't stop this virus."

The car came to an abrupt stop outside the door. In front of the home was a large fountain. No water was flowing, but it must have been quite the sight. Farther down was a parking lot that was filled with three trucks.

"Does he own those, too?"

Jake squinted, killed the engine and got out. "No, I don't recognize them." He cupped a hand over his eyes to get a better look while opening the door. "Hand me the gun and stay in the vehicle."

Kate watched him crouch down and shuffle up to one of the windows. He peered in, and then continued to the next. This time, however, he ducked back and pressed his body against the wall. His nostrils flared and she could see he was trying to figure out what to do. He was mouthing something to her but she couldn't quite make out what. Kate stepped out of the vehicle, then she heard him.

"Go! Go!" he waved with his hands as he rushed towards the vehicle. Not wasting a minute both of them got in the car and he started the engine just as the door opened and an armed man stepped into view. Jake hit the gas just as bullets punctured the vehicle multiple times. The vehicle shot forward, Jake swerved to the right around the circular driveway and cut across the field to a second exit. Behind them, Kate could see in her mirror three men firing at their vehicle. All of them had semi-automatic weapons.

Jake had his head ducked down as they tore out of the long driveway, skidded right and gunned it down the road. Jake pulled into a road that came off the main vein, and he drove into another driveway as if he knew where he was going.

Out of breath and panting hard, Jake brought the vehicle to a stop.

"Where the hell are we?"

"A friend of mine lives here."

They exited the vehicle and raced up to the house. Jake banged on the door, then went over to the window and glanced in. Before he returned, the door opened and a grizzled man, looking to be around two hundred pounds with a duck dynasty beard answered. He didn't initially see Jake so he raised a handgun at Kate.

"You better get out of here."

"Riley!" Jake shouted.

Jake came into view and the man's hardened features smoothed. "Jake? Damn, you are a sight for sore eyes." Before Jake could tell him to stay back because he figured he could be infected, Riley rushed forward and hugged him hard. When Jake eventually pried himself loose from his bear hug, he continued.

"Okay, okay, get off, you big fool."

"Seriously? You're working security now?"

Jake pulled at his uniform. "Was."

"Jake, you back for good?"

Jake kept her distance, wary of being infected.

"Just here to check in on my parents. Riley, have you heard anything?"

"No. Should I have? I've been locked up here for the past few months only venturing out to get food."

"A group of men have broken into my parents' house."

Riley gave a nod and looked past them. "I guess you should come in."

Jake hesitated even though he'd already been hugged. Riley noticed and smirked. "I'm not infected."

Weary from the long drive, both of them entered and were led into a gorgeous living room. A small fire was on to keep the house moderately warm.

"Where's your sister?"

His chin dropped to the ground. "She's gone and so are my parents. I buried them in the yard." A few tears welled up in his eyes and Kate felt sorry for him for a few seconds until she pointed out the obvious.

"You went near them?" Kate asked.

"Oh no," he motioned towards the back window and Kate went and had a look. Outside was a large plastic tarp that covered a large section of the lawn, beyond that was a mound of earth.

"I covered them in a tarp, tied off the ends and dragged them into a hole."

"So you did go near them?"

"No."

His answers were just confusing. Something about the way he spoke seemed a little off. It was almost childlike.

"They died outside?"

"No. Inside."

"I'm sorry to hear that, man," Jake said.

Kate backed up, making sure not to touch anything. Even though they were still decked out in biohazard gear with masks and goggles, she was wary about staying anywhere there might be a chance of contracting the virus.

"Don't worry, they died a long time ago. If I had

contracted it I would have been dead by now."

He stoked the fire and they took a seat on a leather couch across from him. On an oak table in front of them was a bowl of chips, a can of Pepsi and several packets of beef jerky. He offered them some and Kate was tempted, but she passed.

"What did they look like?" Riley said, chewing off a piece of dark meat.

"Like some serious pissed off dudes. Riley, are you telling me you have not had anyone visit or attempt to get into this house?"

"Nope, then again, there are lots of properties around here that look better than ours." That was an understatement. The home almost looked historic. It had to have been at least a hundred years old.

"How do you know each other?" Kate asked.

"I used to date his sister," Jake said with a smirk before turning serious again. He was bothered by the men at his parents' home, and rightfully so.

"Did you see your parents?" Riley asked.

"Nope. Just four guys."

"Well you can stay here if you want. I could use the company. It's been a month since the family passed on. I've thought about heading out of town, you know, looking for help but the thought of getting stuck out there. Nah, here I can live for at least another few months."

"You've got food beyond what's on the table there?"

He laughed. "Of course. My mother was big on buying at Costco. Everything in bulk. She swore by it. Come, I'll show you."

He led them down to the basement where he had two white freezers. One was empty, the other one stacked to the brim with frozen fish, meat, veg and dairy products.

"And weapons? You still got them?"

"Hell yeah."

Kate tossed Jake a confused look. They wandered further down in the basement, through another doorway and then entered what looked to be a man cave. Leather couches, big screen TV, football memorabilia lined shelves, a basketball net mounted on the wall, along with a dartboard and a pool table.

He went over to a brown cabinet on the wall, which was locked, he pulled out a key from a ceramic vase on the side and unlocked it. Kate expected there to be rifles and handguns inside. Nope. Not even close.

There was a hunter's bow, ninja stars and a samurai sword.

"Are you kidding me?" Kate asked. For a second, she had her hopes up that he might have been able to give them another gun. Her nerves were fried after what they just went through.

"What? These beauties are collector's items."

"Great, maybe we can trade them in exchange for our lives," Kate muttered before walking off.

"What's up with her?"

"Don't even ask," Jake muttered. Kate wandered around the room, allowing them some space to discuss whatever harebrained idea Jake had. As much as she could have gone her own way, she felt indebted to him. The only reason she was alive was because he had come to her aid. Otherwise, she might have just bled out on the floor of her apartment — just another casualty.

"Okay, Kate, Riley and myself are going to head over to the house, see if we can't find a way in. There might be a chance they are gone."

"Let's go."

"No. It's best you stay here. With your arm and all."

"No offense. I'm not staying here."

"What? There's chips, more than enough soda, and you can read a book for an hour or two," Riley chimed in.

"If you're going, so am I."

The decision was made. It wasn't that she couldn't have stayed in the house. She didn't want to. Right now, her only chance of getting home was that vehicle and wherever that went, so would she.

They exited the home and decided to make the journey back to the house on foot. Of course, they didn't leave until Riley had geared up. While he was doing that, Kate had to know.

"What's the deal with the ninja stars?"

Jake smirked.

"When we were kids, he always wanted to own them. He had this mad fascination with bad Kung Fu movies. He envisioned himself as some kind of Jackie Chan. Anyway, we used to go to all these conventions. Honestly, that man cave of his was way worse ten years ago. It was filled with marital arts posters; the guy had every Chuck Norris DVD that was out there. Look, I know it seems odd but there are grown adults dressing up in Dungeons and Dragons gear out there, running round like idiots. Well, maybe not now, but there used to be. Riley is pretty mild, really."

Kate eyed him and smirked.

"So, I guess you could say that Riley has dialed it back as he's got older but hey… a guy likes what he likes."

"Good to know," Kate muttered as Riley stepped into view. He had the samurai sword on his back, the ninja stars across his chest and the bow strung over his shoulder with a handgun in his holster.

"You gonna play us a tune with all that shit?" Jake muttered.

"Yeah, yuk it up. You'll be thanking me later."

"You mean, you actually learned to use it instead of drool over it?"

"Don't make me tell her about what you used to do on our sleepovers."

Jake went red in the face and opened the door. "Let's go before further embarrassment."

Riley led the way, like a warrior from a bad Chinese flick.

Chapter 12

Hayley had one purpose in mind when she went into Clayton — to explore Kinney Drug Pharmacy. Contrary to what everyone else said, she was pretty damn sure that it had to have feminine hygiene products. The rosy red river had started a few days ago, and they had already used up what supplies were on the island. It was embarrassing trying to tell the others that she needed pads. Fortunately with Meghan going through it at the same time of the month, she'd agreed to tag along, if only to avoid doing further work on the island.

"You honestly think they are going to have any?"

"People don't think about this. Take me, for instance. I'm usually on the ball when it comes to what I need, but the whole thing didn't even register. Too busy thinking about what to eat, drink and how to survive. The last thing I need to get is an infection down there. Besides, I need to pick up a few other things."

"Like?"

She didn't know Meghan well but they had bonded over the past few months. She was the daughter of Fergus McCalan, a family that had moved to the island only a year ago. Prior to that they lived south of Watertown but her father had managed to start a business in Clayton as a Chiropractor. He'd always wanted to live closer to the island where he had a summer property.

"Like, condoms."

She let out a laugh.

"What?" Hayley replied back. "I'm not getting pregnant in this world now. No way in hell am I bringing a child in to this hell hole."

"I wasn't laughing about that. What about Ella?"

Hayley's brow furrowed. "What's she got to do with it?"

Meghan shrugged, stuck her hands in her pockets and glanced off.

"Come on. Come out with it."

"Well, it's hard not to notice that she's cozying up to

Gabriel."

Hayley nodded slowly as they trudged on towards the building that was just off James Street on the south side of town. She wasn't blind to it. Ever since they'd met in Queens he'd been giving her the eye and spending more time with her. Every time she approached him about it, he blew her off, said she was overreacting. She knew him better than that. That was part of the reason she wanted to visit the pharmacy. Perhaps the whole place had already been looted, but she was going to find out.

"Glad I'm not the only one who noticed. I thought I was losing my mind, being overly possessive."

"Uh, guys change. They think with their dicks. Today, you are breathtaking, tomorrow, you are suffocating. You know how they are. And let's face it, Ella isn't exactly a troll."

"I know. That's the problem. I wouldn't mind it if she was a bitch, at least then I would have a reason to hate her, but she's so…" Hayley searched for the word.

"Nice?"

Hayley nodded in agreement. As they got closer to the one story pharmacy, a few vehicles were parked outside. To the right of it was a car wash and a restaurant called The Castle and Grill.

"We should check out the restaurant. Maybe they have some tubs of ice cream. I would die for a bucket, and well, if it does come to light that your guy is screwing Ella, you might need a tub or two to get you through it."

Hayley slapped her on the arm and she let out a laugh. "Good point."

They kept their wits about them and scanned the area. Across from the Pharmacy was a large school.

Meghan tapped her and started running. "Race you."

Now whether it was a lack of entertainment, not having access to the Internet or just plain old boredom, but she burst into a sprint, chasing after her. When they both arrived out of breath, they laughed.

"I haven't done that in a long time."

"Yeah, you forget the simple things when you spend every waking minute with your nose stuck in technology."

Hayley pushed her way in through a gap in the door. "True."

They spent a few minutes searching around for any product that might have been left but there was nothing. Someone had already been through the place. Tubs were overturned and the remnants of what was once candy floss flavored ice cream was smeared all over the floor. There were several boot prints in it.

"Find anything?" Hayley asked.

"Nah. Though I did find this."

Hayley looked up in time to see a dark mass soaring through the air in her direction. She jerked to the side just in time. A dead rat landed hard. It's body frozen in one position.

"Meghan," Hayley shouted. A roar of laughter came from her.

"You should have seen your face."

For a second she was about to go off on her, but then she let it go. It was what she liked about her. The past two months had been a huge strain on them all. Staying lighthearted when the world was pressing in and forcing them into uncomfortable situations meant everything now.

Back outside, they made their way over to the pharmacy. Metal shutters still covered the windows, and large warnings spray painted in red made it clear in no uncertain terms that they were to enter at their own risk.

Another sign on the outside said.

FLU SHOTS GIVEN DAILY

"You know if Frank catches wind that you visited here, he will go berserk."

"No he won't. Because I aim to bring him back some of his anxiety meds."

They stood in front of the sealed off pharmacy looking at the warning.

"I'm not sure this is a good idea."

Hayley ignored her and started walking around the structure, looking for a way in. It seemed to make sense that they would have sealed the place up like Fort Knox at the onset of the pandemic. Besides stores that catered to food and water, people would have tried to stock up on medicine.

Yet for the most part, others would have stayed clear of it if the sign about flu shots was anything to go by. People would have feared that the place was germ infested and that the only people who would have visited the place were the sick. Hospitals, doctor's offices, and pharmacies were all considered hot spots. The worst places to visit in a pandemic, but her personal needs overruled what fear she had of contracting.

"Over here," Hayley said, motioning to Meghan to join her around the side. Someone had already attempted to get in around the back.

"They must have used a crowbar."

The metal was bent back at the bottom, leaving just a small opening. Fragments of glass were scattered as Hayley got low and shone her flashlight inside. It was daytime outside, but inside, pitch dark. Just on the outside of the door was some dry blood. It looked as if someone had cut themselves on the way in, which meant there was a chance it came from someone who was infected.

"You still want to go in?" Meghan asked. She definitely didn't want to.

Hayley didn't like it one bit, but the alternative wasn't pleasant. Currently she was using a mooncup, which was a silicone hypoallergenic cup that carried about a day's worth of blood and then could be emptied. Some of the other women were using menstrual sponges made from natural sponge. As for the painful cramps, she was using natural willow bark plant in a tea. It basically acted like an aspirin. It tasted like shit but did the trick. Beyond that was raspberry leaves, but they had recently run out of those.

"Screw it."

Hayley got down on her belly and squeezed through the gap. Both of them were wearing N-95 masks and biohazard suits, which made it a little tough to squeeze through as it kept getting caught on the metal, but Hayley was determined. A minute later, she was in. She shone the light around and noticed that the shelves were still stacked. Some of it had been taken, but not everything. Hayley breathed a sigh of relief, got down on her knees and peered back outside.

"You want to come in?"

Meghan looked around nervously, then looked back at her. "Okay."

She was reluctant, but it was better than being stuck outside by herself.

Over the course of the next fifteen minutes they went through the store filling a plastic bag with as many items as they could. It felt like they had struck gold. The pharmacy had been there for two months and while someone had finally ignored the warning and got the nerve to go inside, they hadn't ransacked it, which meant they either were just one person or they planned on returning for more supplies as and when needed.

"I can't believe they left all of this here."

"Well we aren't going to be able to haul it all out."

"Sure we will, once we let the others know."

Hayley held up a packet of gummy worms.

"Medicine isn't the only thing they stocked."

Meghan's eyes lit up in the glow of the yellow light. Hayley tore it open and they polished off the entire packet off without a thought to saving any. There were more than enough packets still hanging on a hook near the counter. Kinney Drug stores didn't just carry medicine. It was like a one shop for everything you need. Pool gear, toys, candy, chips, house products, milk, the whole nine yards. Hayley couldn't believe that Frank had passed over this place just because it had a warning on the outside.

"I think whoever sprayed that warning on the front was the same one that broke in."

"How so?" Meghan said, stuffing more barbecue chips into her mouth.

"They had covered up the hole with a section of drywall. It was almost as if they were trying to keep it hidden."

"Well they are going to be shit out of luck when they

show up here next time."

Hayley cracked open a Red Bull and downed it.

"Did you find any, by the way?"

She twisted around and pulled up several boxes of tampons, and a few packs of condoms.

"Durex Maximum extra-large?"

She grinned. "What can I say? He's well endowed."

Meghan chuckled. "But XL?"

Hayley didn't answer her. She spotted something across the other side of the room. She placed her can down and got up and headed into the makeup isle.

"Oh, sweet baby Jesus." She returned to her bag and started loading it with makeup and shampoo products.

"You can't take all of that. Just the essentials."

"These are the essentials."

Meghan went over and tried out some of the lipstick. They went back and forth spraying different sprays on and relishing the aroma. That's when Hayley saw a staff exit door on the far side of the room.

"I'm going to see if they have a washroom here, change

my pad and well..."

"Enough said," Meghan piped up while continuing to try on different products. Hayley left her bag. She was nervous about what she might find on the other side but as they hadn't heard any noise, they assumed the place was empty. Since being in there they hadn't smelled decaying flesh, but then again, the hole in the door might have vented out some of the smell.

Hayley pushed through a doorway and found herself in a corridor. To the left was a set of stairs that went up to a fire escape, to the right was a lunch room and farther down was a bathroom. She carried a box of pads and entered the bathroom. Instinctively she flipped the switch, but of course nothing happened. "Stupid," she muttered.

A few minutes later she had cleaned up with wipes and added in a new pad and was feeling better. She tossed the old one in a trash can and was just in the process of heading back to the main room when she heard voices. There was no shouting, but it was loud enough that she could make out there was more than one person.

She reached the door and cracked it open just a little and her eyes flared.

Two people had hold of Meghan. One of them was holding a large knife to her throat while the other carried a bat in their hand. They were both dressed in black, and wearing black balaclavas.

Trembling, she reached for her gun but then realized she'd left it with the rest of her belongings. Shit! Her eyes went to the bag lying nearby, her Glock was lying on top. She could hear them muttering something to Meghan but couldn't tell what it was. The one in front of her shone a light on her face and that's when Hayley could see how scared Meghan was. Hayley barely registered it as she was dealing with her own nerves. She was terrified. Do something! she told herself. Her head shook ever so slightly. She was frozen.

"Taking what's not yours?"

It was a female voice. The girl in front put a knife up to Meghan's eyes and Meghan squirmed within the grasp of her partner.

Hayley's eyes darted to the gun on the floor. Go on, you can reach it. She pushed the door ever so slightly, hoping that it wouldn't creak. Had it creaked on the way in? She couldn't remember.

She'd just managed to get it open enough that she could squeeze through when she witnessed the unthinkable. They slit her throat.

Meghan's eyes bulged in her skull, then darted to her. They must have caught it as the one holding her looked Hayley's way. Her nostrils flared and Hayley turned and bolted up the stairs that led to the fire escape. Behind her she could hear them yelling. Her heart was pounding in her chest as she ascended the steps two at a time. As she reached the top, she burst out onto the roof and scanned around. Shit, how do I get down? It was just a clear drop. Maybe ten feet high.

She heard the sound of boots beating on the steps.

They were coming.

Slipping over the side of the roof, she hung for a

second and then dropped.

Her ankle twisted as she landed with a thud. Hayley let out a cry and gripped it but didn't stay on the ground.

"There she is," one of them yelled, peering over. Hayley scrambled to her feet and hobbled as fast as she could away from the parking lot heading towards the school across the road. They fired several rounds at her but missed. She turned back to see where they were, but they were gone from the roof. With her pulse beating rapidly and the image of Meghan's throat being slashed, she hurried across the green, turning back every few seconds to see if they were coming.

When they came into view and started to give chase, tears started to stream down her face. She didn't want to die. Who were they? Why were they doing this?

Chapter 13

Hayley sliced her arm as she thrust her body through the front entrance that had thick shards of glass jutting out. A cry, a whimper, and then only the sound of her boots as she rushed through the darkened hallways of Guardino Elementary School looking for a place to hide. It was a large two story brown building with more than enough places to hide. Frantically her eyes scanned the rooms. She tried several but they were locked. Casting a glance over her shoulder she heard them shouting.

"Which way did she go?"

"You go that way."

Next came the sound of a metal being dragged along stone.

Hayley rushed up to the last corner she came around and took a peek. Sure enough, a little way up the next corridor, the silhouette of a figure could be seen ambling down the corridor looking through the door windows.

"Come out, come out, wherever you are."

Hayley did her best to remain quiet as she shuffled down the corridor to the next corner. She moved around it and her eyes widened. At the far end, another one was holding what looked like an award, taken from a cabinet on the wall. They tossed it and smashed what little glass remained in the cabinet.

Hayley pulled back just as they turned her way. Stuck in a U-shape corridor with two of them heading her way from either side, she was petrified. Her eyes scanned the walls, floors, lockers for anything that could be used as a weapon. There was nothing. Darting towards the gym, she slid inside just as she heard their boots approaching. They'd heard her. Closing the door behind her quietly, she walked backwards, keeping her eyes on it. That's when she saw some skipping ropes in a bin off to the side. She rushed over and grabbed several and took them to the door and tied them around the handles to hold the doors together. No sooner had she done it than a loud bang against the door pushed it in. They were trying to force their way in. Fortunately, the rope kept the doors from opening. They could only open a few inches and from within the gap she saw a person's eye staring at her.

"Little pig, little pig, let me in."

"Go away!" Hayley screamed. She heard them laugh.

For a second there was silence, then they continued tormenting her.

"Then I'll huff and I'll puff and I'll fucking rip your throat out."

They began banging on the doors, and then she saw a knife come through the gap in the door and begin hacking away at the rope.

"Why are you doing this?"

They didn't reply. She turned to run towards another door in the corner of the gym only to see a figure emerge holding what appeared to be a fireman's axe. They raised it and smacked it against their hand. Hayley put her hands up.

"Look, you don't have to do this. I know people that can help."

The rope snapped as the other person cut it and burst through the door holding a large bowie knife. Hayley let out a cry and began begging for her life while continuing to walk backwards until she stumbled over the bleachers. Moving backwards, she ascended them one step at a time trying to stay away as they taunted her. One of them swung the axe and brought it down on the ground, while the other slashed the air.

"Look, I can give you whatever you want."

"Oh, you will."

"What do you want?"

They stopped walking towards her and stared. One of them pulled off her mask and smiled as it dawned on Hayley who it was.

"What do we want?" There was a pause. "Blood."

Right then in that moment, they rushed her and she raised her arm in one final act of self-preservation, but it was pointless. The sharpened steel cut through it like a warm knife through butter. A piercing cry echoed in the gymnasium, only to be followed by more as they hacked into her flesh until all that could be heard was the dripping of blood from the bleachers to the ground below.

* * *

It was the sound of distant gunfire that made Frank stop. He raised a clenched fist and the others listened. A few more shots and he figured it was coming from the south. Mark had told them that they were going to visit the Pharmacy, and even though Frank had been adamant about avoiding it, Hayley went against his wishes. It was to be expected with more people on the island and no one stepping up to be a leader after what they went through with Butch. Everyone was just doing what the hell they liked.

"Keep up," Ella shouted. She was several yards ahead.

They couldn't have been more than three or four blocks from where multiple shots could be heard. Ella was the first to rush forward. Though Frank called out to her to slow down, nothing was stopping her. The sense of impending doom hung heavy over them as they sprinted down James Street. When they emerged near the Pharmacy, Frank scanned the field, the restaurant, and car wash but there was no one to be seen.

"Ella. Wait!"

It was too late, she had already disappeared around the corner of the building. One by one they piled into the Pharmacy after her. Frank heard Ella's cry long before he squeezed through the gap. When he finally rose to his feet and brushed off the debris and glass, he spotted what she was gazing at. Lying in puddle of blood was Meghan. Her throat slit from ear to ear. Frank pulled Ella back and she sobbed in his arms for a few seconds and then pulled away.

"Hayley!"

Gabriel had already darted out back with Zach and was exploring the rooms. Frank followed them and made his way to top of the roof where Gabriel was staring out shaking his head. "Where did she go?"

"Gabriel," Zach said, pointing to a patch of blood on the lip of the wall. They leaned over to see if she had fallen but she wasn't below. That's when Zach slapped him on the arm and pointed. All three of them looked out across the street and field in the direction of the school. Two figures emerged and glanced their way. For a few seconds they stared and then broke away into a cluster of trees.

"Gabriel!" Frank said grabbing his arm but he was already half way over the wall and about to drop down. "Wait!"

"Get off me, man," Gabriel said. Frank released him and he dropped down and broke into a sprint.

"Go with him," Frank said to Zach. While they shot off towards the school, Frank trudged back down the stairs feeling out of breath, out of shape and wishing that people had listened to him. It wasn't just about avoiding infection, but sticking together. That's how they would survive this. The country had become a desperate place. Frank pushed back through the doors to find Ella kneeling down beside Meghan's body, tears streaming from her eyes. In the short time on the island, the two of them had bonded. Meghan was the type of girl that got along with anyone. She was helpful and kind like her father. The thought of informing her father, Fergus McCalan, about her death was going to be beyond hard. He only had one child, and he'd lost his wife the year before to cancer. It was going to devastate him.

"We need to get out of here. Help me find something to wrap her in."

Frank began looking around and after a minute or two he looked back to see Ella still standing there.

"Ella."

She snapped out of whatever daze she was in and wandered over to where he was. While the store yielded nothing, out back in the storage room was a tarp wrapped around a palette of boxes.

"That could have been me," Ella muttered without even looking at Frank. He was tugging at one corner, trying to loosen some rope that held it in place. He briefly looked at her.

"Meghan had asked me to go with her, but I hung

back to help Sal with the new girl."

"This is exactly why we need to stick together. We can't drop our guards for even a moment. Frank continued untying the rope and then pulled off the tarp.

"Go ahead, say it."

Ella had been pushing back against him over the past two months. She wanted to venture out, go beyond the island and Clayton and scavenge in other towns, but she didn't want to do it with him. He understood that she was old enough to make decisions, but that was before everything changed. Danger was everywhere. It might not have been knocking on their door for two months, but it was out there, just biding its time and waiting for someone to pick off. Meghan had been singled out, her and Landon's family, but by who? The figures they saw in the distance were too far away to see their faces. Were they just the tip of the iceberg? Had a new group moved into the town looking to stake its claim the way Butch had?

Frank shook his head as they returned to Meghan, laid

the tarp down and rolled her body into it. A minute or two later they had her wrapped up tightly. There was no way they were going to be able to get her out of the small gap in the door. It was locked and there was far too much shit outside blocking the entrance to push the door open.

"We're going to have to lower her down from the roof."

Ella grabbed one end and Frank lifted and shuffled backward up the stairs. When they hauled her body out, they sat it down to take a breather.

"Where did Gabriel go?"

Ella turned her head and received her answer without Frank saying a word. Trudging across the field with her body in his arms, Gabriel and Zach returned. Gabriel was covered in blood and any attempt by Zach to help was brushed off. Frank and Ella lowered Meghan's body over the edge to the ground and dropped down.

Tears flowed down his face as Gabriel lowered Hayley's bloodied body on to the hood of an abandoned car. Her right arm was missing, and she had a huge gash in her skull, and multiple stab wounds to her abdomen. Gabriel crouched down and Frank placed a hand on his shoulder.

"Zach, there's another tarp inside. Can you get it?"

He nodded and headed around. No words were exchanged. For what could be said? Frank was at a loss on how to deal with this. It brought an array of emotions to the forefront as he recalled the trouble they encountered with Butch.

When Zach returned, Frank asked him if they saw anyone nearby, but he shook his head and proceeded to try and wrap up Hayley's body.

"Leave her alone," Gabriel said.

Zach stopped.

"Gabriel, we need to take her back, give her a proper burial."

"This is your fault," he muttered in a low tone.

"What?"

"If you had just checked out this place, she wouldn't have gone in."

"Gabriel," Zach said. "You can't blame him."

"No? Who can I blame?"

Ella stepped forward and put an arm around him. "This isn't the time to point fingers, Gabriel. Do you think Hayley would have wanted that?"

He scoffed. "Don't act as if you knew her."

Ella scowled and backed away. He was hurting and looking for a way to lash out. Frank motioned for Zach to continue but Gabriel was having none of it. He rose to his feet and pushed Zach back. "No, I'll do it."

The tension between them was tangible as he hoisted Hayley up. Her body draped over him in a fireman's lift. He wouldn't let anyone else touch her and though he struggled on the way back to the dock and had to set her down a few times, he refused help.

As they came over a rise, Mark, Tyrell and Tom sprinted up to meet them. Their faces were a mask of horror and shock. Gabriel lowered her body into the boat and no sooner had he released her, than he lunged at Mark and gave him a right hook to the jaw. Mark stumbled back and landed hard. It took both Tyrell and Frank to hold him back from continuing.

"This is your fault as well. Why did you let them go?"

Mark lay on the floor, rubbing the side of his face. His lip was cut.

"Huh?"

"Gabriel, please. Just get in the boat," Zach said. He shrugged both of them off and hopped into the boat, causing it to bounce around on the water. They all stood there for a few minutes trying to calm down and get a grip on the situation, but there was still someone out there killing, and they would kill again if given the chance.

"Let's go," Frank said, motioning for the others to climb into the boat. He cast a nervous glance around the empty marina before pushing the boat away from the wooden dock.

All the way back across the water he tried to think about what to say to Fergus. And yet nothing came to mind. Nothing that would suffice, heal or bring comfort.

To lose a child before passing on was just plain wrong. There were no two ways about it. If anyone might have been able to relate to him, it would be Sal. And yet the loss of his wife and daughter had caused him to retreat into a shell. He'd barely spoken to his surviving son, Adrian. Jameson had been looking after him along with his own daughter, Kiera, while Sal had tried to work through his grief.

* * *

Jameson was there to greet them when they docked. His eyes flitted over to Frank. Ella could tell that he was full of questions. He tried like the others to help Gabriel with Hayley, but was only met by an angry reply.

"No!"

As others came over the rise and it was learned that others had died, Sal emerged, along with Fergus. A look of horror and utter despair came over him as his eyes fell upon the body of his child.

"No. No. Baby!" He repeated the words over and over as he dropped to his knees and his face turned a harsh red.

He didn't care about the blood that was getting on him from her cut throat. He nuzzled his face in the crook of her shoulder and sobbed loudly. Ella looked to her father, realizing that he would feel the burden of responsibility, and yet it wasn't his to carry.

"Another child?" Sal muttered before tossing Frank a look of disgust.

Chapter 14

"Jake, are you sure about this?"

They had been squatting in a patch of trees a short distance from Jake's home. For the past ten minutes, they had been surveying the property and trying to determine the best course of action to take. Kate had been attempting to talk Jake out of it; Jake had been trying to get Riley to calm down. She was beginning to see that he must have been a handful. He was a grown man with the mental capacity of a twelve year old. Obviously it wasn't his fault, but it was liable to get them killed. She couldn't see the benefit of bringing him along. He stuck out like a sore thumb, and standing beside Jake he reminded her of Lennie Small from the film Of Mice and Men — except for the fact that he had a samurai sword attached to his back, ninja stars across the front of his chest and a gun in hand.

"I have to know if they are alive."

"I don't mean that. I mean," she nodded to Riley, who was beginning to worry her. He just didn't appear to be in the right frame of mind. Was he even aware of the danger, or assuming that this was all part of some elaborate game that Jake had concocted?

"He might be a little slow, Kate, but he has got my ass out of some of the worst situations when I was a kid."

"Like?"

Jake looked off towards the house, trying to avoid answering the questions.

"Jake! Like?"

Reluctantly, he began to recount a story from his youth about being bullied and how Riley stepped in and took out both of the guys who were laying a beating down on him.

Kate placed a hand over her face. "That was bullying. This is real life, Jake. Those men in there are armed." She cast a glance over to Riley. "We should take him back."

"I'm not going back." He'd overheard. "I know how to fight."

"No one is saying you don't, it's just…"

"That he's slow?" Jake asked. Kate's head sunk. Perhaps it was the mother in her. The need to make sure that everyone was safe, or maybe it was the fact that Riley didn't look like he was taking this seriously, but she didn't feel good about it. They had already nearly been shot. She didn't think she could handle the guilt if Riley got injured.

It didn't matter what she thought. Jake had made his mind up.

"Riley, circle around the right side of the building, I'll go left."

Jake was about to rush off when Riley grabbed him by the arm. "Hold on, here."

He opened a bag and pulled out two devices which resembled walkie-talkies, but they weren't your typical kind. No, these were blue, and had the faces of smiling dogs on them. Kate frowned, and Jake looked embarrassed as he accepted one from Riley.

"What the hell are those?" Kate asked.

Jake cleared his throat and tried to spit the words out, but they came out in a mumble.

"What was that?"

He grit his teeth and then leaned towards her. "Paw Patrol Walkie-Talkies."

Kate might have laughed if the situation had been anything but serious, but was this guy out of his friggin' mind? Riley rushed off through the trees, heading around the right side.

"Look, don't say anything. It's hard enough having to deal with it myself, but…"

"Why didn't you tell me he was mentally challenged before we got to his house?"

"Because I figured you might object."

"Object? This is serious shit, Jake. He could get killed. Do you want that on your conscious? He thinks this is a game."

"I know, but as crazy as it sounds, he was damn good at this game when he was a kid. I'm telling you. He might be challenged, but he's a smart guy."

Kate wasn't too sure how to resolve the two. Challenged but smart? She had grown up with a father who saw mental illness as a weakness. That's why after she met Frank, she hid the fact that he had a phobia from her father, otherwise there would have been no way in hell he would have given them his blessing. It was absurd, really, but in some ways, she had to wonder how much of her father had rubbed off on her.

Kate nudged him. "You should get going."

"You okay staying here?"

"Don't have much choice. One of us needs to keep an eye on the front."

Jake smiled, then in a crouched position darted away until he was out of sight.

* * *

Jake circled the house, his eyes drifting over the windows, looking for any sign of the men. So far there had been no movement. He shot out of the tree line and rushed towards the back of the house. At the back of the home there was a large koi pond, a porch with a few

Adirondack chairs and a clear shot of the kitchen. His heart was thumping inside his chest as he reached the porch and stayed low. Out the corner of his eye he spotted Riley. He had to blink twice to get a grip on what he was seeing. Not only had he covered his face in green army camo paint since he'd seen him last, but he was now climbing up the side of the house using the drainpipe.

Jake made a sound with his lips trying to get his attention but he couldn't hear him. He tried the walkie-talkie but the damn thing didn't work. *Oh, my god, this was a bad idea,* he thought. Jake twisted around and peered over the window ledge into the kitchen. Two men sat at the breakfast counter scoffing down some food from bowls. He eyed one of the men's guns on the counter beside him. The other was in a holster. Shit!

Scrambling across the ground, trying to stay out of sight and not make any noise, he made his way over to the far end of the porch to see where Riley had gone. He was considering going up the pipe which led to the second story. From where he stood he saw a bedroom window open. No, don't go inside, that wasn't what he had chatted over with him. They were going to wait until one of them stepped outside and then overpower them.

A sound of gunfire got his attention.

It came from the second floor, which could only mean one thing — they had spotted him or Riley had fired upon them. Jake pulled the magazine from his gun, and checked how many rounds he had left. There were nine bullets. He hurried towards the back door and without waiting a second he burst in. The two men were already up and heading for the door when he caught them off guard. In those seconds, it was like time slowed. He felt like a fly stuck in honey. He brought the Glock up with both hands and unloaded three rounds. The first struck the guy in the chest, the next in the head, the third caught the other guy in the throat. Both fell back against the wall, sliding down and leaving a smear of blood against the wall. Jake moved fast through the kitchen, into the hallway, then ducked into the living room. There was no one in there. The front door was open. Another gunshot resounded upstairs, three more, then one outside. Jake rushed to the front entrance to find a body on the ground with two ninja stars in the back and blood seeping out a wound in the abdomen.

Concerned for Riley, Jake raced back inside and double-timed it up the staircase.

"Riley!"

When he reached the top of the stairs, he found Riley on the ground with a bullet wound to his side, and another to his right chest. He was still alive but choking a little on blood. His eyes drifted to a pair of feet sticking out from another room. Jake rushed to his side and dropped down.

"You're going to be okay, buddy."

"Did I do good?"

Jake nodded. "Yeah, you did good."

He looked as if he wanted to say something but the words never escaped his lips, just a shallow breath, then he stared forward. He was gone.

"No."

Jake slumped down beside him. The sound of boots pounding the stairs and Kate's voice made him look towards the staircase. She emerged, her head turning from side to side until she spotted him.

"Jake?"

She got close and then looked down at Riley, she leaned forward and ran her hand over his eyelids to close them.

"Dumb idiot went completely against what I told him."

She wanted to say she told him so, but that wouldn't have helped. Instead she checked the rooms in the upper part of the house. They were all empty, except for the bathroom. Inside, slumped in the bath were two bodies. An older man and female. Both had been shot in the head. It was his parents.

She turned back to Jake who was still reeling from the death of his childhood friend, and though she didn't want him to endure any more pain, she had to tell him.

"Jake," she said in a soft voice.

He glanced sideways.

"They're dead."

She thought that might prevent him from taking a look, but it didn't. He rose from the floor and staggered over to the bathroom. He placed a hand on the frame and looked inside. A rush of emotion hit him and in that moment he broke down. This guy who had been so fearless in coming to her aide in Atlanta unraveled before her eyes. He slumped down to his knees and dropped his gun and began to sob.

Kate didn't know what else to do but place her arm around him and sit.

* * *

They didn't move from that spot for close to an hour. Once he was all out of tears he sat there staring at the wall in an almost catatonic state. Unsure if he was liable to do harm to himself she stayed with him, even though she was concerned that whoever the men were, perhaps there were others. The smell of iron, salt and dampness permeated the air. Eventually Kate had to get some air. She was feeling nauseous surrounded by the dead.

"We should go downstairs. We can deal with this in a minute. Get some air."

"No." He shook his head. "I need to deal with it now."

Jake got up and pulled down the shower curtain and began trying to heave his father's body into it. He cast Kate a glance, but with only one arm free there wasn't a lot she could do to help. Still, she tried to assist and eventually they got both his mother and father out onto the ground. Kate went and got some sheets from off the main bed and brought them in. They spent the next ten minutes wrapping the bodies and then dragging them down the steps. A feat which was not easy. Riley weighed a ton. Once they had dragged them outside, Jake went about gathering a shovel and digging graves. While he did that, Kate searched around in the kitchen for some food. Fortunately the place was well stocked with beans and canned items with which she was able to piece together a meal for the two of them. She glanced down at the two dead men in the kitchen and wondered how long they had been eyeing the place. How common were home invasions becoming now that survivors were feeling the strain of the pandemic? What happened to morals? Did anyone have them? Were they cast aside the moment people felt their stomachs growl? Did they abandon their humanity or were they always like that? The fact was humanity had always been hunters and gatherers, and yet over time as technology improved and companies set about making people's lives easier and better, people became civilized. At least, that's what most would assume. But being civilized only seemed to work under certain conditions. Once law and order went by the wayside, all that mattered was staying alive. And people were prepared to do whatever it took.

Jake came in, covered in dirt. He rubbed a soiled hand across his face, leaving a big black smudge mark, and he collapsed in a chair and began to sob again. It was difficult to see him lose so many people within a short span of time. No siblings. No family.

She placed a bowl of cold beans and unheated chili in

front of him. It was packed with more sodium than anyone should have, but it was food and right now both of their stomachs were grumbling. If they were going to make it the final leg of the journey, they would need more strength.

"You know, I knew Riley since I was seven years old. I remember being dropped off by my mother at this new school and feeling completely alone. A teacher asked Riley to look after me. Can you imagine that? A mentally challenged kid was given the responsibility of looking after me. Man, did I get hell for that. And yet, you know what, despite all the name-calling. Riley never buckled under it all. It was like none of it affected him." He paused to scoop some of the food into his mouth before continuing. He seemed desperate to tell Kate this account. As if in some way it would help him to cope with the loss of his friend. "Anyway, no one touched me after that." He snorted. "I used to call Riley the big friendly giant. He never once complained and yet he could have easily walked away."

"Sounds like he was a good friend."

"The best. I'm going to miss him. When I left to go to Atlanta he was distraught, to say the least. I promised I would return and even invited him to visit me there but he wouldn't leave his family. That's just what he was like. Loyal in life."

Jake continued eating and finished off what was left. They spent the next ten minutes routing through the house looking for batteries, flashlights, gathering together what little food remained in a bag along with the guns of those who had died, and then packed up one of the trucks outside. All the while he recounted stories from his time growing up. He spoke about his father's love of fishing and how they bonded every summer growing up through camping. He smiled as he talked about coming home from school to the smell of cooked food and his mother's warm embrace. These were all the things that meant the most to him. It wasn't his father's wealth, or the career opportunities his father could have given him. It was his relationship with them that made him who he was today.

Jake siphoned the other vehicles' gas into a canister and tossed it in the back.

"You ready to head out?"

Jake nodded while giving one final look at his home. "Bye, Mom. Bye, Dad. Bye, Riley."

Chapter 15

Chester breathed in deeply as he arrived in Clayton, New York. It was late afternoon when they reached the deserted town. A light breeze blew newspaper along the street like tumbleweed, a dog darted out of an alley nearly causing him to slam on his brakes. It barked a few times and then vanished around a corner. Chester rested his elbow on the window frame, one hand on the wheel while the other smoked a cigarette.

"Smell that."

"Oh god, you didn't let one go again did you?" Roy said bringing his window down. Roy and Beatrix rode shotgun while Sawyer and Bobby were huddled up in the back of the truck. They had taken turns ever since leaving the cottage. The journey had been uneventful. Chester thought he would encounter more resistance, people desperate for food, firearms, gas, hell even a cigarette, but the roads had been quiet. Occasionally they saw another vehicle pass by but there was no attempt at stopping them. People were being cautious, playing it safe. It was the smart thing to do. He needed every bullet he had and he sure as hell didn't want to get into a war with others before dealing with Talbot.

"No, it's the sweet smell of revenge."

"I swear you have lost your mind, Chester," Beatrix added.

"If I did, that explains why I invited you and not Tex or James."

She scoffed and went back to looking out the window.

Sawyer tapped on the window behind them and Roy slid it open.

"Please tell me you have the address for this guy and that this wasn't all just in vain."

Chester leaned forward while keeping his eyes on the road and reached into a space that was usually reserved for coins. He retrieved a scrap of gray paper and held it up. Scribbled across it in black ink was both Frank's and Sal's home addresses.

They headed for Jane Street. Frank's home was located at the very end on the right hand side. An American flag flapped in the breeze outside. It was a grey clapboard home that wasn't big. Chester felt a wave of excitement as he got closer. The look on his face when Talbot saw him was going to make this trip that much sweeter. The first thing he noticed when they pulled up outside was there was no vehicle in the driveway.

"Now listen up. Roy, Sawyer, I want you both to go around the back. Beatrix and Bobby, you go either side of the house. I don't want him escaping and I can assure you this guy is a slippery little bastard. When you hear me unload one, let it rip. You got it?"

They all nodded.

Chester killed the engine, hopped out of the large 4 x 4 Ford and pulled out from the back of the truck his Mossberg 500 Tactical shotgun. It had a 5 + 1 capacity and an 18.5" barrel. He'd been biting at the bit to use this ever since he'd purchased it a few weeks before everything went to shit. He shouldered it; getting it real comfortable before he strolled up to the house, aimed it at the lock and unloaded a round. He wasn't in the business of knocking, that shit got your killed, and gave people time to escape. He wasn't going to give him even a second to react. Wood burst and glass shattered as the others unleashed hell on his house. By the time they were done, the walls were peppered with holes.

After reloading, Chester reared back and gave what was left of door one hell of a kick.

"Move in!" he yelled to the others. Bobby and Beatrix came around the front while the other two went in the back. They moved swiftly through each of the rooms checking under the beds, looking in closets, inside cupboards and even in the basement. Nothing!

Chester grit his teeth.

At least if Frank's virus infected corpse had been lying on the ground he would have been satisfied that he died a painful death. He certainly had one in mind for him. It wasn't just going to be a gunshot to the head. No, that would far too easy. He was going to draw it out, make him suffer and plead for his life. Then, and only then would he put him out of his misery. By that he meant he would disable him by firing two rounds into his kneecaps, and elbows. Next to contracting the virus, there was only one other thing worse — being unable to defend, scavenge and survive, and he planned to rob him of all his faculties. He wouldn't show mercy this time. That well had dried up the moment he spat in his face by setting alight his vehicle. The moment the country abandoned law and order. Now it was his law, and he was about to restore order.

* * *

Misty was still relishing the murders they had committed long after she watched the light leave that girl's eyes. She washed her hands in the sink using bottled water they had gathered from a home on the east side. They were holed up now in the home of Sal Hudson. They had been there for a few hours hoping that the others they'd seen would follow them back or at least pay the place a visit. After killing four people and two children, she didn't feel anything. Even as she made those kids climb up on to that barrel and she kicked it out from beneath their feet and watched them dangle until they went limp, she felt no empathy. In her mind, they had robbed her of her family. Butch meant everything to her. The way of life they had established on Grindstone brought a comfort that she hadn't felt growing up.

Until she met Butch, her life was full of couch surfing, struggling to make ends meet and days of binging on alcohol to numb the pain of her past. She stared down into the sink, watching the blood wash off her hands. It brought back the memory of the night when she was only thirteen years of age. Her stepfather at the time was prone to drinking and the arguments in the home were intense. It was when he crossed the line and hit her that her mother stepped in. Up until that point, her mother had always justified her reasons for letting that bastard stay. *He will change. He's having a bad day. I haven't done enough for him.* Misty had heard all the excuses. It eventually caught up with her one night when her stepfather returned and in a drunken rage, grabbed a knife off the counter, and stabbed her to death. Misty saw the whole thing take place. She still had the scars in her shoulder from where he'd attempted to kill her before several neighbors broke in after hearing her screams and stopped him. Had they not come to her aid, she would have joined her mother. Now, as she looked back, she kind of wished she was dead. This was no life. Without Butch, she had nothing. She was back to square one in her mind.

She had met Butch when she moved to Clayton at the age of nineteen. She was waitressing and fell for his charm. Though he came across as a hard man in front of others, she knew that was just an act.

Misty dried off her arms and leaned back against the kitchen sink as Rachel entered the front door.

"No. They are gone. They took the bodies, as well."

She'd sent her out to see if they were still around.

Misty scoffed. "Sentimental fools."

She said it but on the same hand, she was the same.

After returning to Clayton from the Canadian side, they had located Abner's place of residence and found Butch's body lying against a boat. She buried him not far from the property and spent several hours beside his grave sobbing. That was when she knew that there was nothing left for her. She had placed her gun against her own head and contemplated joining him. But it was Rachel that stopped her. She gave her a reason to live — revenge. Though she was riddled with guilt and anguish, she knew Rachel was right. If she took her own life, Frank and the others would have won. And she was wasn't going to die that way. It felt like Butch was speaking to her from the grave. His words whispered in her ear, giving her the strength to finish what he had started.

"You okay?" Rachel asked, noticing that Misty looked distracted. Misty blinked hard.

"Yeah. So, what did you say?"

"I went back over to the school. Weren't you listening?"

"Yeah, sorry."

"So, what now?"

"They'll come looking."

"And you really want to stay here? What if they bring others?"

"We're not going to stay here. Just tonight. Our best bet is to keep moving around. Keep our eyes on the island. They'll show up eventually."

"And if they don't? What if they decide to only scavenge on the Canadian side?"

"Then we'll go there."

Rachel glanced down at her own hands that were covered in blood.

"Are you having doubts, Rachel?"

She shrugged. "I mean. Killing those kids. I just thought we were going to scare them."

Misty walked over to her and grabbed her by the shoulders. "Do you remember what Randall looked like? His skin burned? Do you think for one moment they showed him an ounce of mercy?"

"We've killed six people, Misty, and we're still alive.

We've made our point. Why don't we just leave now?"

Misty stepped back and frowned. "And let them live out their lives?"

"No, this isn't about them. It's about you, me, our future."

"There is no future, Rachel. You've seen it yourself. There is nothing out there beyond this town. This is it."

"You don't know that."

Misty leaned back against the counter and stared at her. "So where would we go?"

"Maine. We could meet up with Bret."

"Bret is a coward. I wouldn't share the same air space as him."

"He just wants to live. Don't you?"

Misty picked up a bottle of water and chugged it down. "Everything good about my life is buried beneath the earth. Whatever dreams, aspirations, or goals that I had about the future are dead. There is no coming back from this pandemic. The only thing I want now is to make sure those bastards pay for taking Butch's life."

"Then what? Huh? What then?"

She shook her head slowly. "I don't know, perhaps I will go through with putting that bullet in my head."

"You think Butch would have wanted that?"

"Butch would have wanted this. That I know. Look, if you want to leave, the door is there. I'm not going to stop you. But when you have made it out of town, I hope you can sleep at night. Because all I see is Butch, all I hear is him telling me to avenge his death."

"You know how insane that sounds, Misty?"

Misty chuckled. "Not nearly as insane as thinking that you can survive out there on your own."

"I won't die just so you can feel better about what they did. Butch is gone. I get it. It hurts. I miss Randall every day, but he's gone. Nothing I can do can change that."

"Of course there is." Misty got real close to her. "Don't tell me for a second you didn't enjoy cutting that girl's throat."

"I didn't."

"No? Because I never told you to do it."

"She was struggling. She could have…"

Misty smiled. "Just face it. You are as fucked up as I am. That's why you're still here. You need me just as much as I need you."

She shrugged and shifted her weight from one foot to the next. "Maybe."

Right then, they heard the sound of a truck drawing near. Misty darted to the window and looked out. She couldn't tell who was inside but she was pretty damn sure it was them.

"Go upstairs, now," she said.

"No, let's get out of here," Rachel said. "We can take them out from a distance. I'm not getting trapped in the same house."

"You're not understanding. This is perfect. Go upstairs now."

They hurried up the steps, Misty tugged on a thin cord that was wrapped around a piece of metal on the ceiling, a hatch opened and wooden stairs appeared. She pulled them down and they made their way up into the attic.

Misty retrieved them and closed the hatch just as the door opened downstairs.

* * *

It smelled like cow shit inside. Chester burst in through the back door, prepared to unload a few rounds. He kicked a chair over and slammed the butt of his gun into a fish tank full of stale water. It cracked and water gushed all over the floor.

"Alright, tear the place up."

The others spread out tearing photo frames of the walls and firing a few rounds into the large TV. Once they were done, Chester stood outside to have a cigarette. He was beginning to think that the trip had been a pointless endeavor, although he wouldn't tell the others that.

"Where the hell are they?" Roy asked, showing his frustration.

"How the hell am I supposed to know? Perhaps they're dead."

"Let's go. Let's leave this place."

Chester turned to him and scowled. "You think I came all this way to leave?"

"Look Chester, I know you want this guy dead, but maybe he didn't return. Maybe he just went back to Queens or somewhere else?"

"No, not this guy. A man who leaves his home to collect his daughter values family. He wouldn't leave his home. He's here. I can feel it."

"Okay, maybe Beatrix is right. Perhaps you have lost your mind."

Roy was about to leave when Chester grabbed a hold of him and threw him back into the house. "If any one of you doubts me. Speak now." He pulled his firearm out and waved it around in the air. "That bastard Frank Talbot is around here somewhere. I'm going to find him with or without your help."

"Chester, as much as I want a piece of the action, what if Roy is right? What if he's not here?"

Chester was about to respond when a female voice came from the corridor. "He's here."

All of them turned fast, bringing up their weapons towards a pint sized woman who had her hands up.

"Woh! Hold on, you kill me you are going to be searching for a long time."

"Who are you?" Chester asked, his forehead pinched tightly.

"The name's, Misty Guthrie and this is Rachel. Now, I don't know why you want him, and quite frankly, I don't give a shit, but I know an opportunity when I see one. You help us and we will help you."

"Give me one reason why we shouldn't end you right now?"

"Because I can show you where Frank and Sal are."

Chester looked at the others and grinned. "Well, lead the way."

Chapter 16

The survivors were looking for someone to blame. Crammed into the tiny hall, the atmosphere was stifling. Tom had gathered together anyone who wished to discuss the current string of deaths. It was a recipe for disaster. There was already a rumor spreading that people were tired and restless. It was to be expected. Life wasn't getting any easier. Society had become used to independent living and retreating into concrete castles and hiding behind technology when things got tough. None of that could be done now.

They were like crew on a ship. Everyone had to chip in and help, and when one suffered, they all did. Though Tom was against telling them that someone was picking them off one by one, or that Landon's children were hung, Frank felt honesty was the best policy. Attempting to hide the truth would only make them an easy target.

Frank squeezed into the corner, observing, but saying

nothing. Outside in the darkness, rain beat down against the tin roof. Its rhythm almost lulled him into a trance, as the noise of arguing got louder.

"You must know who did this!" Janice Ekhart stabbed the air with her finger.

Tom put his hand out to try and calm the situation. It was like being inside a pot that was gradually reaching its boiling point. They wanted answers and Tom was struggling to find words to appease them. He looked over to Frank, as if hoping that he would take over. Sal sat with Eva, who had gravitated towards him since returning to the island. He glanced at Frank and looked away. The situation between them had gotten worse. It was as if he blamed him for the deaths even though he knew that Frank had tried to persuade Landon to stay.

Donald Garrat stepped forward and prodded Tom on the chest. "I say we go over there now and deal with this matter."

Tom stumbled back as four more of the families agreed.

"Look, this is not the way to handle this."

"It worked before, didn't it?"

"Well, yes, but…"

"No more 'buts'. If you aren't going to do anything, then we will."

Donald stormed towards the door. He was a few feet away when Frank unloaded a round into the ceiling. The crack silenced the rowdy crowd.

"No one is going anywhere. It's dark out. They have already killed six of us. We don't know how many of them there are, or what kind of firepower we are going up against."

"Who the hell are you to tell us what we can or can't do?"

Frank pushed off from the wall and walked over to Donald. "You want to go over there and get stabbed to death, then by all means, go ahead. But I'm telling you right now, no more people have to die. There is a reason why they attacked them in Clayton and not here on the island. Either they don't have a boat to get over here, or they are waiting for people like you to get riled up and venture over there. Then, one by one they are going to pick you off just the way they did with the others."

"We'll take our chances."

Donald grabbed the door and Frank slammed his hand against it.

"You go over there, don't come back."

He released his grip and Donald scowled. "I own property on this island and you don't get to tell me what to do. We had enough of that with Butch, we won't put up with it again. Now get out my way."

Frank hesitated for a second then stepped to one side. Donald exited the building taking with him four more men, one of which was Fergus, Meghan's father. He could hear him out there telling them to gather up ammo. They were going to leave for the mainland in fifteen minutes. ATVs growled to life and tore away into the night.

A brief period of silence followed.

"Anyone else eager to die?" Frank asked before exiting

the building. Ella caught up with him. "You're not going to let them go by themselves, are you?"

"I'm not a babysitter."

"No, but you have spoken on behalf of us all. They respect you."

He chuckled. "Yeah, that looked like respect back there. Look, it's not my place to tell them what to do."

"But people look up you. After what you did."

He smirked. "Are you sure about that? Because from the rumors being passed around this island, it appears that people are divided, tired and ready to leave. Why the heck do you think Landon left? He had already filled their heads with the belief that we could go back to living."

"Maybe we can."

"Oh God, Ella, not you as well."

Rain cut through the night, plastering their hair to their faces.

He trudged back to his ATV and straddled it. He was about to start it up when she placed her hand on the key. Water poured off her face.

"Listen Dad, this island is no safer than the mainland. We all know that. The fact that we were able to take over is proof. Now if there are ten, twenty or more people over in Clayton that have their eyes set on this island, then they are going to find a way to get it."

"Your point, Ella?"

He was growing tired of hearing everyone's great ideas. He yearned to be back on his own island in his own space. He understood the others were the same. It was what was driving them to want to leave. It was the reason Donald and the others wanted to put a stop to anyone who was killing people. It wasn't because they gave a shit about Landon or Hayley. People were restless. There was this grand assumption that once folks got used to living without the luxuries that modern day society provided they would be happy, fulfilled and would no longer crave what they had before, but it was all a lie.

He missed waking up to the sound of waves and silence. He missed frying up bacon and sitting out on his porch in the mornings, drinking coffee by himself. Now all he heard was people grumbling and complaining.

The truth was society had the attention span of gnat.

"At some point we need to move on from here."

"Move on? If I'm moving on, it's to that island over there," he pointed across the water to what once was his haven from society."

"So, you're going to let them go by themselves."

"It's evening. It's dark. If they want to risk their lives, then let them."

With that said, Frank started up the ATV and tore away.

* * *

On the mainland, Misty gazed through the night vision binoculars for a few seconds before handing them to Chester. They had been watching the island for the better part of thirty minutes.

"So, tell me again. Why do you want him dead?"

"He killed my husband and his cousins."

Chester lowered the binoculars and glanced at her. "And how many survivors are on the island?"

"Fifteen, maybe twenty. There could be more now."

He snorted. "Okay, then I guess we will wait for them to come to us."

He handed back the binoculars and returned to his truck. Misty jogged up to where he was with a look of concern. "Well, I was thinking we could go this evening, cross over in the dead of night, slit their throats. I know the island like the back of my hand. We could..."

Chester turned and placed a finger against her lips. "I said we would work together. I didn't say that I would do what you wanted. If we do this, we do it my way."

"But..."

"No 'buts'. There is a reason your husband and his cousins are dead, and a reason why two of you managed to kill six of them. Look, I know you are hasty to bring the hammer down, so to speak. But these things require patience. We'll take residence in a home close to the water. Somewhere that provides us with lots of cover but at the same time enables us to keep an eye on the water."

"Oh, I agree. Heck, that's what I initially had in mind

before you guys showed up. But now with more of us, we can take the island."

"Because they did?"

"No, I just meant…" Misty trailed off.

"Do you know how long I have been a police officer?"

She shook her head.

"Since I was nineteen years of age. It's all I have ever known. As hasty as I was to join the police and get out there and solve crime, I came to realize that it's all about timing. You can't rush these things. There were times when I was a rookie that I just wanted to bust into houses and break a few heads, but that would have got me killed, much like the way your husband was killed. A series of hasty choices leads to a series of hasty deaths."

With that said, he turned and got into the truck, and the others hopped in. Misty and Rachel just stared at him.

"Well? Are you getting in?"

Over the course of the next twenty minutes, they searched for a home to stay in. It was agreed that they would divide themselves into two groups. Group A would have Beatrix, Chester, Roy and Misty. They would take up residence on Washington Island. Group B would have Bobby, Sawyer and Rachel on Rivershore Drive near Steele Point. They would communicate by radio. In his mind it was simple. Based on the locations that were commonly used, they would wait for them to arrive. If they didn't arrive within forty-eight hours, Chester would run with what Misty had in mind.

"Do you think it's wise to split up?" Roy asked as they entered a home on Washington Drive.

"If they have already lost six people, they aren't going to take chances the next time they visit. They probably won't use the same dock and they might only venture out in the day. I don't want us all to be in the same location. It's as simple as that."

Chester strolled through the house searching for beer. His throat was parched and he was frustrated with having to explain himself. He was in no rush. The fact that he knew that Talbot was here set his mind at ease. It meant that his visit wasn't going to be in vain. Misty might have been biting at the bit to tear into Frank, but she was going to have to rein in her emotions. The only reason he was keeping her around was because she knew the town and she was a sweet bit of ass. He had every intention of nailing that the second he could pull himself away from Roy and Beatrix.

"Bobby, come in?"

The ham radio crackled.

"Reading you loud and clear."

"Good. Check in every thirty minutes or unless you see something."

"Roger that."

Chester placed the radio down and turned his attention to Misty. She was a slim built woman, flaming red hair and a body that screamed for attention. He glanced at Beatrix who was cleaning her weapon. She practically worshipped that thing.

"Beatrix, Roy, go down by the water. Take the binoculars and keep an eye on any approaching boats. Give me a shout if you see anything."

"Gotcha." Roy grabbed up the binoculars and shot outside. Beatrix, however, wasn't as quick. She lingered for a while and got this smirk on her face before heading out and closing the door behind her. She tapped the air and narrowed her eyes as if she knew what he was up to.

Chester watched Misty from a distance. She was looking out the window. After arriving, Roy had found a few bottles of wine in the basement. They were sitting on the side. Chester picked one up and unscrewed the cap before pouring out a glass. He took it over to her and handed it. She took it and eyed him suspiciously. She wasn't skittish like other women he'd been around; she almost looked as if she understood what he was up to. After the road trip from hell, he was ready to blow off some steam and he couldn't think of a better way than getting his dick wet.

He sipped at the wine and leaned back against a counter. "So tell me about yourself. How long you been in Clayton? Where are the cops? Why didn't you leave after your husband died?"

"I think we can skip small talk, don't you think?" She replied.

Oh yeah, she was on his wavelength. He put his glass down and ambled over to her. She frowned as he took her glass of wine and placed it down, then pressed his body against her.

She allowed him to get close for a second and then he felt her knee slam into his nuts, followed by her pressing the barrel of her gun against the side of his temple.

"I might have lost my husband, but if you ever try that again, I will drop you where you stand."

Slowly, Chester raised his hands. "Excuse me. I must have read the signs wrong."

She scowled at him and grit her teeth. "Yeah, I think you did."

Chester backed up and eyed her with a degree of hostility. Few women turned him down, and the fact that there was a chance that they could all be dead tomorrow, he took the rejection to heart. Misty lowered her handgun and was about to walk away when he grabbed her from behind and twisted her arm around her back, prying the gun from her grip. He pressed up against her and swept her hair back. He traced his lips down the side of her face and across her neck before coming up to her ear and whispering into it.

"So, you like to play games?"

He forced her arm up hard, making her wince in pain.

He reached around for his belt buckle and was about to undo it when the rear door on the kitchen slid open and Roy burst in.

Oh for fuck sake, he thought.

"Chester. Chester. You need to come see this."

"Later."

"No. Now."

He grit his teeth. He was seconds away from doing to Misty what he had done to others while out on patrol. Every fiber of his being was throbbing. He pulled away and took her gun with him. He didn't trust her and he had a strong feeling she would put a bullet in him the first chance she got.

"Now, play nice," he said before following Roy out the door. He heard her mutter something but he didn't catch it.

"There is a boat heading this way."

He peered through the binoculars and took a look for himself. Sure enough, there they were. Was Talbot among them? They were still too far away to see the occupants. He could only make out their silhouettes.

"You want me to get Bobby and the others up this way?"

"No, I have better idea."

Chapter 17

After the pulse-pounding incident in Pennsylvania, Jake had been quiet for most of the journey. They had entered New York State just after ten that evening, and were only a few hours from Clayton. Kate wanted to press on, but they were getting low on gas and Jake looked tired. Emotionally, he was drained. Both of them were, if she was honest.

"We should stop for gas."

"Yeah, right. The past six gas stations were all out."

"So we siphon some from these abandoned vehicles."

Vehicles were in abundance. They were dotted all over the highway. Towns and villages they drove through had more than enough to choose from. Siphoning was the only way they were going to make it. The needle on the fuel gauge was nearly in the red.

"We'll stop in Dryden and see what we can find."

They were about ten minutes from there.

"So what's the deal with you and your husband?"

Kate was driving to give Jake a break. He had a baseball cap pulled over his eyes and his feet up on the dashboard.

"It's a long story."

"Well, this is a long journey. Humor me."

She shook her head and smiled. They passed by several large farmhouses, barns and fields full of unpicked corn. She had to swerve around a huge combine harvester that was in the middle of the road. It was as if someone had attempted to steal it or use it as a means of transportation and had simply abandoned it or run out of fuel.

"We met when I was working for the Armed Forces Health Surveillance Branch as a junior epidemiologist. Like most relationships, it started off well. Back then, he was a different man. It took him a while to open up to me about his disorder."

"Disorder?"

"He suffers from what is known as Mysophobia. It's a pathological fear of contamination and germs."

Jake lifted his hat and cast a glance her way. "Are you serious?"

"Very much."

"Well, he can't be dealing with this very well."

"No, I don't imagine he is. However, according to him, he's made progress. What that means, who knows?"

"I guess if there was ever a time to face your fears and overcome them, this would be it."

Jake snorted and it was the first time she had seen him smile since Pennsylvania. If sharing her life story was going to help, then she didn't mind. It had always been a sore point with her. Her parents had stayed together and well, she just assumed that her marriage would work. In many ways she felt like a failure. What hurt the most, though, was having Ella watch it all unravel.

A vehicle shot by them going at least ninety. It was heading out of the town they were about to pass through. Jake peered over his shoulder and all that could be seen were two red glowing lights disappearing into the distance.

"They were obviously in a hurry."

"Um," Kate mumbled to herself. "Perhaps we should take a different road. The last thing we need is to run into more trouble."

"I don't think taking a detour is going to matter. Trouble is everywhere. People are hungry and scared. Anyway, let's not get off the topic, this was just getting good."

He nuzzled his back into the leather seating and waited for her to continue.

"Well, we divorced and went our separate ways. That's it."

"Hold on a minute. Back the train up. How did it lead to that? Like how long were you married and did he cheat on you?"

"No, he never cheated. I mean, his eyes wandered from time to time but don't all men's?"

"I guess so. Hard to enter an art gallery and only gaze at one painting."

She chuckled. "Well, I've never heard it put that way."

"Well, you know how some people get. Folks get too riled up about what this guy did or that girl did. I mean, what did they expect? Monogamy is a tough pill to swallow. Sure it's all rosey at the start. It's always good at the start but boredom sets in, couples piss each other off, they start to notice each other's quirks and no longer find them adorable. Five, ten, hell, even twenty years later they are digging the bottom of the love barrel just trying to figure out why they got together in the first place."

"So you're not a one girl kind of guy?"

"Hey, I didn't say that. Maybe if the right one came along."

"Oh, so it depends on the right one?"

"Yes. No. I mean. Sort of."

She laughed.

"What I mean is that it involves a lot of variables. Timing. If you get married too early, you might just be too immature to deal with the responsibility that comes with it. If you get married because of faith and then that changes later in life, you are now dealing with two different people than the ones that walked up that aisle. And well, it just goes on and on. I think what I'm trying to say is that marriage is overrated. If you love someone, why do you need to put a ring on it?"

"Beyoncé would beg to differ."

He snickered.

"Like, can't two people just live with each other, enjoy each other without the need to announce to the world that they are an item? Hell, I used to get so sick of seeing people filling up my Facebook newsfeed with what they were doing with their spouse or partner. It seemed like everyone was out to prove they were in some loving relationship, when in reality they probably wanted to throw up every time they saw them."

Now it was Kate who was smirking. He had a point. Perhaps it didn't apply to everyone, but there did seem to be a need for some people to try and prove they were in a loving relationship.

Kate ran a hand through her hair before gripping the wheel again. "Well, those days are over. No power. No

Internet. No Facebook updates. So I bet you're as happy as a lamb."

"I am. I never even owned a phone. I couldn't be done with it. If someone wanted to get hold of me, they could swing around to my apartment or write me a letter. I mean, what happened to the days when folks used to write to each other or see each other in person? Now all people do is text. It's impersonal. No wonder the world is plagued by selfies and butt pictures on Instagram. Everyone is clamoring for attention. I mean seriously, people are out of their minds."

She snorted.

"So you expect me to believe you didn't own a phone?"

"I did until my girlfriend broke up with me. After that I ditched it."

"You never did tell me why she broke up with you."

They were getting close to the town. A dark green sign for the Village of Dryden flashed past them, just a blur in her peripheral vision.

"Oh don't even get me started on that girl."

"Now come on. You wanted to hear about my marriage, I want to hear what led to your break up?"

He smiled and readjusted his position on the seat. "First things first, you have to finish what you were telling me."

They were heading down a hill. On either side were towering pines and homes nestled into the woodland.

"It just didn't work out. It's as simple as that. How does any relationship end? We had a fight and I told him I was leaving him. He promised to change but I'd heard that before. I couldn't do it."

"Was it just that?"

"No, it's never just one person."

"Oh I don't know about that. Nancy sure knew how to push my buttons."

"And you didn't contribute?"

"Maybe I did but, you know what, I helped pay her way through college."

"You did, or your father?"

He nodded and leaned forward, squinting into the distance. Outside, the only light came from a canopy of stars and the odd light that lit up a home.

"He paid. But the principle is the same. She waited until she had completed her education before she booted me out. I came to find out two weeks later another guy had moved in. I mean, who in their right mind rebounds that quick?"

Kate didn't say anything. Her relationship with Tom had developed long before her marriage ended. He was attentive when Frank was absent, considerate when Frank wasn't. Relationships were complex. Rarely did people finish a relationship and then sit a year before diving into another. Loneliness kicked in. A need to feel valued. It was messy and there wasn't exactly a guidebook.

"So you think she was with you for the money?"

"Oh, without a doubt. And Frank? What about him?"

She didn't immediately reply. Kate contemplated the question. Frank had his faults, but there was never a time that she didn't feel loved. The times he was present, he was caring. The times he wasn't bothered by his OCD, he was considerate. Perhaps she had overlooked the good in him.

"Well—"

There was a loud pop sound, then instantly Kate found herself wrestling with the steering wheel for control. The truck veered sharply to the left. Jake was thrown towards her then back again as she tried to keep the tires on the ground. A bottle full of water and several bags hovered in the air momentarily before landing hard. She jammed the brakes, pumping them steadily and doing her best to keep it from crashing, but it was virtually impossible. For a split second she thought she had it, then it was gone. The truck veered off the road, went over a rise and turned on its side. How many times it flipped was unknown as Kate's head struck the side of the truck, and then it was lights out.

* * *

When she awoke, the wheels were still spinning and the horn was blaring. She clenched her jaw and pried her body away. The horn stopped and she breathed a sense of relief, even if it was short-lived. Her body ached, and she felt as if her leg was broken but then realized it was just the way Jake had fallen on her. He was out cold. She ran her hand over his neck and could still feel a pulse. A trickle of blood ran down her cheek. The windshield was cracked, and the side windows shattered. Glass and debris were everywhere. Pieces of the surrounding bushes were sticking into her and water from the river was filling up the inside of the compartment. She tried to get out from underneath Jake, but she was stuck.

"Jake. Jake!"

He didn't respond. More cold water rushed in, chilling her to the bone. The taste of iron filled her mouth, and she wiped her face with the back of her hand. Think! She twisted in her seat and unbuckled the belt. Once unhooked from her restraint, she found she had a little more room to maneuver. The sound of rushing water only scared her. She didn't want to die by drowning. A virus would be a tough way to die, but drowning? No, that was not going to happen. She'd always had a fear of water, it was the reason why she didn't agree to Frank's idea of living out on the island. Of course, she never told him that.

Kate grasped at the seat, her fingers tearing into the old leather, trying to pull herself out from underneath. Slowly but surely she managed to get free, that's when she was hit with the real pain. She screamed in agony. A piece of twisted metal had embedded in her lower leg. The more she tried to move the more it dug in.

"Oh God," she yelled. Right then, Jake came around. He groaned and he looked up.

"What happened?"

His eyes drifted over the mess and the water rushing in.

"We need to get out now."

Jake hauled himself up. He had a large cut on his forehead and it was bleeding pretty badly. Droplets of blood dripped down onto Kate. "Give me your hand."

"I can't move, there is some metal stuck in my leg."

He looked down and then moved into a position which would allow him a closer look. He sighed. "I can get it out but it's going to hurt like a bitch."

"Just do it."

Kate reached for a piece of leather and tugged it free and placed it between her teeth. "You ready?"

She nodded and mumbled the word "yes" but it just came out garbled. Clenching her eyes shut, she waited for him to tug on the metal. When he pulled, she bit down as hard as she could and screamed. He held it up. "It's okay, it's out."

As the vehicle was on its side and water was gushing in through the front windshield, the only way out was to go up through the passenger side window. Jake climbed his way up. Kate saw that his shirt was torn and he had a large gash down his arm. He reached for her and both of them struggled to climb out of the waterlogged death trap.

"Oh hey, wait. My gun."

Kate turned and reached for the rifle that had been

resting on the back of the seat but was now jammed between twisted metal. She gave it a hard pull and returned to exiting the truck.

They stumbled over the lip of the door and found themselves lying on the side of the truck. Slowly they made their way across to the rear of the truck and landed on the bank. It was mushy and wet. A deep rivet was in the soil where the truck had cut into the earth as it slid down the side of the bank. Both of them were soaked to the bone and shivering.

A few minutes later they had made their way up to the road.

"What the hell happened?"

"I don't know. One second I had control, the next there was a loud pop and I couldn't keep it straight."

"Maybe a tire burst?"

"Perhaps."

Kate not only had an injured arm, but now she was sporting a nasty gash in her leg. She hobbled a little and Jake offered to support her. He wrapped her arm around his neck and slipped his around her waist. They looked ahead towards the small village, hoping to find a place to treat their wounds.

They trudged on into the darkness of the night, battered, bruised and cut. The sound of music could be heard coming from somewhere in the distance. Kate hoped it was the military. They had seen them in a few cities now. It gave her hope that perhaps survivors were going to be okay. That eventually, over time, society would rebuild and thrive once again.

Chapter 18

Donald Garrat had spent four years in the military before he was kicked out for insubordination. He went AWOL. Of course, he never told anyone that. He painted a very different picture, one in which he'd been wounded in the heat of battle. Something glorious. The kind of thing that would get him a free round of drinks. It was all bullshit, but who cared? Since his time in the army, he had worked in construction until he retired at the ripe age of sixty-six. He wasn't a young bean anymore, but he had a fire in his belly and he sure wasn't going to sit back and take shit from anyone on the island, especially not Talbot. Who the hell did he think he was? Sure, he had got rid of that asshole Butch Guthrie and his goons, but he would have got around to doing that anyway. It was just a matter of time. Hell, it had been his idea to revolt. Landon was the only one who understood and had he not been killed, a day from now Donald would have been back in Clayton as well. He was done taking orders from anyone else, and he certainly wasn't going to wait until they got picked off by whoever had savagely killed Landon.

He cast a glance at Fergus McClaran. Poor fucker! he thought. He was a shell of a man since losing Meghan. It shouldn't have happened and it wouldn't have if the island had been under his leadership.

They were missing a true leader. Someone who could speak on behalf of them, not just tell them to stay in their homes. He looked at the other two men in the boat, Harry and Warren. This was proof that he could lead them. They had followed him without even second-guessing. They wanted to fight back but were being hindered by that clean freak Talbot and his despondent pet, Sal.

He patted Fergus on the shoulder. "We'll get them, Fergus, don't worry."

"I hope so."

Fergus was the only one he was concerned about. He

wasn't a fighter. The other two looked as if they might toe the line, but Fergus, no. He was house trained, the kind guy that spent his weekends fulfilling honey-do lists. A bitch. There was no other way to put it. The guy just lacked a backbone. Had that been his daughter killed, he would have gone ballistic. No, it was time to nip this in the bud and prove to the rest of them on the island that to get a job done, it required a real man.

The boat spun around, the motor letting out a throaty sound as it kicked up the dark waters and he brought them up alongside the dock on Washington Island.

"Now listen up. You are not to engage unless I say so, do you understand?"

They nodded. He tied off the boat and they hopped out.

"We are going to stick together. No separating. Watch my hand signals. Are any of you familiar with military hand signals?"

They shrugged. "Great. Well, if I do this," he held up a clenched fist. "You freeze. If I do this, you move on.

Understand?"

Fergus mumbled something. Donald grumbled as he got out of the boat. They moved out, keeping their rifles leveled and following Donald through the back of a yard onto Washington Drive. They hadn't made it a few houses down the street when a woman staggered into view with her hands up. She was being pushed forward by a cop.

"Get on your knees."

The cop shouted at the woman and she dropped down in front of him. He pushed the barrel of the rifle against her head.

They were both still a fair distance from them. Donald squinted for a second. He knew who it was. It was Misty Guthrie. What the hell was she still doing there? They had kicked them off the island over a month ago.

He motioned to the others and they approached. Once the cop caught sight of them, he flinched and pointed his weapon at them.

"Who are you?" he demanded to know.

"I was about to ask you the same thing." Donald motioned with his head towards the water. "From the island. What's going on?" Donald asked trying to make sense of what he was seeing.

"The woman here killed several families on the island."

Donald screwed up his face. He was trying to make out the uniform. It was similar to Clayton's police uniform but he couldn't tell if it was one of them. He didn't know anyone in the police department. In fact, he had made it a point to give the place a wide berth because they had pulled him in several times for drinking and driving. The second time he got a ban.

Before he could say anything, Fergus stepped forward.

"I lost a daughter. Did you kill her?"

The woman raised her head. There was an odd look of defiance in her gaze. She snorted and that must have triggered something in Fergus as he rushed over with his rifle leveled at her head.

"Back up," the cop said, pushing Fergus back.

"But you said."

"I said that she is involved in the killing of two families. I didn't say who."

"My daughter's name was Meghan." He lowered his weapon and fished around in his jacket pocket and then retrieved a wallet. From that he pulled a photo and shoved it in the woman's face.

"Did you kill her?"

"Listen sir, I don't know who you are or what—"

"What's your name?" Donald asked the cop. He was skeptical of what he was seeing. There was something about it that didn't add up. He kept his gun focused on the officer.

"Officer Grayson."

"Grayson?"

"You got a badge I can see? An official ID?"

"ID? Why the hell would I have an ID?"

"Do you live here?"

"Yeah, that home over there."

"Number 16?"

He nodded. Douglas's eyes darted over to the home.

"There isn't meant to be anyone on this island. We were told that it was abandoned."

"Well, you heard wrong. Now if you don't mind, I'd like to get back to what was I about to do."

Douglas glanced down at the woman. She wasn't trembling. He'd seen enough victims in the war to know the look of someone who was expecting to die. She was not expecting to die.

"I'm going to need to see that badge of yours."

"What?"

"You heard me."

"Okay, sure."

The man reached behind his back and pulled out a wallet from his back pocket, he tossed it and it slid across the gravel road. With one eye on the cop and the other on the wallet he went to retrieve it. No sooner had he got within two feet of the wallet when a gun went off. He looked up just in time to see Fergus drop to his knees. The next shot that rang out struck Donald in the shoulder. Harry and Warren backed up firing multiple times but it was useless. Several shots fired from behind them and they hit the ground. Donald bolted back towards the boat, gripping his shoulder and firing wildly in multiple directions. He was just trying to buy himself enough time to get out of sight.

As he disappeared behind the corner of a house, he groaned in pain. His hand was covered in blood and he was starting to feel dizzy. A few more shots rang out, bullets snapped over his head and his heart was pounding in his chest.

This was a bad idea. Why didn't you listen to him? He berated himself as he hit the dock and rushed down to…. Shit! Where did it go?

The boat was gone.

Laughter ensued from a distance. He turned to see the cop, the woman and several other men making their way down to where he was. He lifted his weapon but it clicked. He was out of ammo.

"Oh dear, it looks like you are missing a vessel."

"Listen, we can talk about this."

"Talk?"

Donald tossed his gun down and sunk down to his knees. The sound of their boots against the wooden dock as they got closer caused him to tremble. He didn't want to die and yet he knew it was going to happen. He should have seen this coming. The others were meant to screw up, not him.

"My men took the liberty of confiscating the boat while you were gone. I hope you don't mind but be assured I will put it to good use."

The cop got closer to him. Donald didn't look up. He saw his boots get close.

"Go ahead. Do it," he said.

"Do it? Do what?"

"Don't play with me. You're going to kill me. If you're going to do it, just get it over with."

The cop began to act surprised, as if was suggesting something that was outlandish.

"Oh, I'm not going to kill you — at least not yet. Hell, I might just let you bleed out."

"Then what do you want?"

"Oh, that's the million dollar question. What do I want?" He tapped his gun against the side of Donald's head. "I want what's in your head."

"What?"

"What's your name?"

He hesitated and then replied. "Donald."

"Well Donald, how about your tell me how many are on the island over there?"

"I don't know."

The cop tapped the gun against his head again. "Oh, come on, Donald. Let's not play games. Misty here tells me you were one of the locals. How many are over there?"

"Maybe fourteen, could be less, could be more."

The cop crouched down in front of him. "You don't seem very sure. Why is that?"

"It wasn't my job to do roll call."

There was a pause and the cop started to laugh. "Oh, I like that. It wasn't your job." He stopped and gazed intently into his face. "You wouldn't be disgruntled, would you, Donald? I mean, you sound pretty pissed."

"Fuck you."

"I'm so disappointed, Donald. I really thought you were going to be helpful, but…" the cop rose up and sniffed hard. "I guess I was wrong."

Donald didn't even hear the crack of the gun.

* * *

His body slumped over on the dock and Chester rolled him off into the water with his foot. He sighed. "What a crazy fucker."

He turned to speak to the others and was struck across the face with a right hook. Chester stumbled back and then grinned. Misty had her fist balled.

"Don't you ever point a gun at my head again."

He chuckled. "I think we are starting to finally warm up to each other."

The others burst out laughing as Misty stormed off.

* * *

Sal had heard multiple gunshots. They were distant and coming from the mainland. He'd been one of several that had gone down to the dock to try and talk Donald and the others out of going over. It wasn't that he didn't think what they were doing was admirable, or right, even. Heck, if he had his way, he would have gone with them, but he had Eva and Adrian to think about.

Tyrell came into view through a patch of trees.

"Did you hear that?"

"Yeah, it's coming from Washington Island."

"We should inform Frank."

"Why?"

"What?" Tyrell asked, confused by the question.

"Why do you need to inform him?"

"I don't know. He likes to be kept in the loop about what's going on."

Sal turned and lowered the night vision binoculars. He couldn't see a damn thing out there. It was too far away.

"He already knows what is going on. It's to be expected."

"And what if those shots weren't coming from our guys?"

"Then I guess we won't be seeing them in the morning."

Sal turned to head back up.

"What is up with you and Frank?" Tyrell asked. "I know you've lost your wife and daughter, but I don't see how that has to do with Frank."

Sal stopped walking and turned back towards him. His eyebrows rose. "You nearly died and you are defending him?"

"I was wrong, Sal. If I had listened to Frank, that cop would still be alive."

"A cop? Who gives a shit about a cop. My daughter and wife are dead because of the actions of Frank Talbot."

"He was trying to do the right thing for all of us."

Sal approached Tyrell and he backed up a little. "Do the right thing? The right thing was for us to walk away. If we had, they would still be alive."

"But for how long Sal?" Frank asked, stepping out from the shadows.

"How long have you been standing there?"

"Long enough. I came down here because I heard the gunfire."

Sal scoffed and went to walk past him. Frank grabbed him by the arm and pulled him back.

"How long are you going to keep dodging me?"

"Get your hand off."

"Sal. I did what I felt was right for us as a group. If we had done nothing, maybe Gloria and Bailey would be alive. Maybe we could have survived another month, but you know as well as I do, Butch would have eventually made his way over — then what? I didn't light that damn fire. They did."

"But you gave them reason."

Frank scoffed. "I gave them reason, did I? Look, if you are really looking for someone to blame, perhaps you should look a little closer because, let's face it, if you hadn't left to go to Queens with me, you would have been here and perhaps you would have stopped Butch from taking everything I had in stock. That's what started this. Not what I did after. So if you are looking for someone to blame, maybe you should blame yourself."

No sooner had he spit the words from his mouth, when Sal cracked him with the hardest punch he could throw. Frank stumbled back but didn't fall, so Sal charged at him and knocked him to the ground.

"That's it, Sal. Get it out. Get it out." Frank yelled. As he threw punch after punch, Frank didn't defend himself. He allowed him to unleash a flurry of jabs and hooks until his face was bloodied and Tyrell was pulling him off.

"Sal. No more."

Sal rose up and shook his head. Frank had just allowed him to go nuclear. Why? He could have easily beaten the shit out of Sal but he never moved. Sal gazed down at his bloodied hands and they trembled. He was becoming something he wasn't. This wasn't him. Gloria wouldn't have wanted this.

He staggered back, ashamed.

Frank rolled to one side and spat a mouthful of blood out. "I'm sorry, Sal, that they are gone. I would trade places in a heartbeat if I could, but I can't change the past."

Tears formed in Sal's eyes as Frank struggled to get back to his feet. What was happening to them? They were coming apart at the seams, buckling under the strain.

Chapter 19

A giant sign loomed over them. It was called the Pony Express Motel. The neon lights weren't on, but there was light coming from the office. A Victorian style house was off to the left, stairs snaking up to the porch. Both of them gazed at it. There were several lights flickering inside. No vehicles were outside and there was no one in sight.

"Okay, that is just downright creepy."

"Reminds me of The Bates Motel."

"Well, just don't take a shower," Jake said as they hobbled towards it. In the distance they could see a gas station and restaurants, but they weren't in operation.

"Perhaps we should just keeping going," Kate said.

"With your leg like that? Not until we get it bandaged up. Anyway, who knows, maybe they have a working bath, hot food or even a bed for the night. After the shit we just went through, I think a little bit of R&R is in order."

"I'm not staying here overnight. We are only hours from Clayton."

They kept moving towards the office. Outside was a bench, a mosquito catcher buzzed nearby, letting off a blue glow.

"If you are in a hurry, we can be there by seven — that is of course if we can find a working vehicle. If not, we'll get there when we get there."

They stumbled up to the office and Jake leaned Kate against the wall as he opened the door. There was no one inside. A candle flickered on the counter, casting ghostly shadows against the 1980s style flowered wallpaper. Everything about the place looked dated. An old rocking chair was off to one side. It smelled musty. Above him were water strained ceiling tiles. Against the right wall was a stack of tourist pamphlets offering discounts.

"Hello?" Jake yelled, expecting to find the owner had stepped out back. He passed by a long mirror and caught a glimpse of his ragged appearance. His shirt was torn and covered in blood, his hands were covered in grime, his face dirty and he had a large gash on the top of his head. He touched it and winced. He walked over to the counter and looked down at the logbook. He spun it around and noticed that no one had booked into the place in over two months. There was a cup on the side and he noticed steam was coming out of it. He touched it, then smelled the contents. It was coffee. Warm coffee. Someone had to be nearby.

"Okay, looks like no one is here, let's go," Kate said from outside, stumbling forward and trying to leave.

"Hold up. We're not going anywhere. There is cup of coffee on the side. Someone is here. Let me go check the house."

"Jake. No, please don't do that."

It was dark, late and the whole appearance of the motel had upped the creep factor to ten.

"Look, it will be okay. Just take a load off your feet over there, and I will be right back."

"Famous last words."

"Kate."

"I'll come with you."

"Not like that you won't. I don't want to have to support your weight up those stairs."

"Are you implying I'm fat?"

He chuckled. "No, just… sit, stay."

"I'm not a dog."

He rolled his eyes and mumbled, "I think I can see why your husband divorced you now."

She glared at him, not finding his remark amusing. Jake didn't stick around to get an earful. He jogged off towards the house, leaving her alone. She shuffled over to a bench and took a seat. She kept a firm grip on the rifle and looked around nervously. Jake arrived at the door and gave a firm knock. He looked back at her and mouthed something but she couldn't hear. The wind was picking up and her entire body was shivering. She desperately wanted to get out of the wet clothes, take a bath and slip into a warm bed. She was hungry but the pain in her leg was worse.

The door opened and an elderly lady answered it. Jake appeared to be explaining their situation as he would point to Kate, then somewhere else in the distance. Probably, telling her that they had crashed. She gave a nod and invited him in. Jake turned back and smiled, then entered the house, closing the door. Great! He was probably going to have a warm meal, get cleaned up and then come and get her. By that time she would be frozen to the bench.

"Can I help you?" a voice said off to her right.

She didn't even hear him approach. Standing by the door that led into the office was an older man; he couldn't have been more than fifty five years of age. He wore round spectacles and was dressed in a brown pair of pants and a cardigan. He almost looked like Mr. Rogers.

She flinched a little, startled. "Sorry, I didn't hear you approach."

The man looked around and returned to staring at her, waiting for her reply.

"Um, I'm Kate and my friend Jake just went up to

your home. He's inside."

"Inside?"

"Your wife invited him in?"

"Wife?"

Okay, his answers were starting to make her nervous. She kept a good grip on the rifle and moved it slightly as if to give him fair warning. He noted her movement.

"Oh, Anna, yeah, my wife." His eyes dropped to her leg. "You're injured."

Ten points for observation, she thought. The lower half of her leg was soaked in blood.

"Come, I'll have Anna take a look at it."

Kate hesitated.

"I'm not infected. Are you?"

She shook her head. "No."

Kate rose up and the man gave her a hand. "What's your name by the way?" she asked. Please don't say Norman, please, she thought.

"Harold."

It took them a few minutes to climb the steps but

when they reached the top he opened the door and called out for Anna. Jake turned and quickly came over to help. Once inside they beckoned them into the kitchen. It had a country feel to the place. A wooden plaque on the wall had the Lord's Prayer. That put her mind at ease. They were religious folk. Kate took a seat at a table and Anna went and filled a bowl with water. She had graying hair and looked a little worse for the weather.

"How are you managing to cope?" Kate asked, trying to break the ice.

Anna gazed at Harold. "It's tough but we are scraping by."

Harold was busying himself in one of the cupboards. He returned with a tray that had a box of crackers on it, and scoops of sardines.

"It's not a lot but I'm sure it will help."

"Oh really, you don't have to do that."

"No, it's the least we can do."

Jake didn't object, he lifted his N-95 mask and immediately started tucking in, one hand scoffing down the fish and the other gulping down mouthfuls of water. Anna came around and pulled out a pair of scissors. She cut up the pant leg around the cut and rolled the pant back. She took a cloth and began wiping it down. The bowl of water soon turned a nasty red and she carried it away.

"So where are you folks from?"

"Atlanta."

"How is it there?"

Jake replied while eating. "Not good. Real bad."

He shot out two word answers while shoveling the food down as fast as he could. At the rate he was going he'd have indigestion later or would toss it all up.

"And whereabouts are you heading?"

"Clayton," Kate replied. "My family is there."

"Ah, that's a long way from Atlanta. May I ask why you were there?"

"She worked for the CDC," Jake spat out before Kate could answer. She didn't like telling people where she worked, especially after this had happened. It would conjure up images in their head and cause them to make assumptions about her and right now she preferred that no one knew.

"The CDC, is that right?" Harold said, leaning back against the counter, folding his arms. "So you would have been familiar with this pandemic, yes?"

Kate nodded. "My work dabbled in it."

"Dabbled?" Jake said. "Tell the truth. You were trying to find the cure."

Both Anna and Harold looked intrigued. Great, how many questions were they now going to ask? She tried to shift the conversation away before they got carried away.

"So do you have any other family?"

She thought she caught Anna smirk as she washed out the bowl and wiped down the side. "Two grandchildren and one son."

"Oh, they around here?"

"My son is working on one of the rooms at the moment."

Kate found his answer strange. Why on earth would

someone at this time of night be working on a room when they didn't appear to have anyone staying or anyone that would stay. Motels were a magnet for germs. It was part of the reason why she didn't want to go near the place, though she was sure Jake thought it was just fear. It was partly that. They had to be careful. After seeing that vehicle shoot by them on the way in, she had to wonder what had spooked them, or maybe they hadn't even stopped in the village.

"And the others?"

"Asleep. You'll see them in the morning."

Kate rose up and tried to see how her leg was. It was painful but she could walk on it. There were no broken bones but there had been a nasty chunk taken out of her leg.

"Oh we don't want to put you out," she said, moving towards the door.

"Oh, you wouldn't be doing that." Harold said, moving over to the door. He almost looked as if he was trying to block her way.

"Sit down, Kate, you haven't even eaten," Jake muttered. "Unless of course you don't want it. In which case I will have it."

"Yes, come," Harold guided Kate back to the table as if she couldn't do it herself. She took her seat and picked at the food. Jake studied her like a hungry animal.

"Go on dear, eat up."

She picked up a cracker and bit into it. It wasn't crunchy. Stale more than ever. She really wasn't fond of sardines and being as they weren't in the tin, she wasn't too sure she wanted to eat it. It was quiet in that kitchen and over the course of the next few minutes Harold peppered her with questions about the virus. What was it? Had anyone contracted it and survived? Did they have a cure? What type of research was being done into finding the cure? Could she cure it? She did her best to answer him but for all her answers it didn't seem to satisfy him. There was something not right about either of them. They were a little too perky. Everyone else they had met so far were either complaining or were ready to kill. Not once had they asked them what kind of supplies they had. Sure, they had walked onto their property with just the clothes on their backs, but weren't they curious about the vehicle?

Kate eyed her rifle leaning up against the wall. She took her time eating and yet with every bite she was feeling more uncomfortable. Both of them were staring at her and then looking at the fish.

"Aren't you going to eat the rest?" Harold asked. "It will give you strength for the journey."

Jake was leaning back in his seat as if he had just worked his way through a thanksgiving turkey. He had this grin on his face, oblivious to the fact of how strange these two were acting. Or maybe it was just her? Kate had her guard up ever since being attacked in her apartment. They weren't dealing with ordinary folks anymore. Just desperate and slightly crazy individuals who wouldn't think twice if it meant they survived.

She pushed her plate away, and Anna frowned. "Well you need to eat, my dear. Can't let that go to waste. Not now."

"I already had a few things to eat before we arrived."

Jake tossed her a confused glance. He knew they hadn't had anything since that morning. She narrowed her eyes, hoping he wouldn't say anything. He didn't. Instead, he pulled the plate over to him and went to tuck in. He had scooped up some of the fish on to a fork and was about to throw it back when Anna took the fork and plate from him.

"Now, let's not be greedy."

"Oh right. Yeah."

"Come, we'll show you to your rooms."

Jake went to get up and he stumbled a little. "Oh, man I feel tired."

"Probably that long journey," Harold said, taking hold of him and guiding him down the hallway and up the stairs. Kate noticed Anna was sizing her up. "Come on dear, let's get you tucked in for the night."

Another odd thing to say but she shrugged it off and followed her upstairs. There were four rooms, and a large bathroom. The floors were hardwood and polished. All the way up the stairs dotted on the walls were old photos, none of which seemed to show any of Harold and Anna. Anna led her into a room where there was a large four-poster bed. It smelled musty.

"Here we go. If there is anything you need, just give me a shout."

She closed the door behind her and she heard what sounded like a key go into the lock. That was followed by a clunk. Kate went over to the door and tried it, thinking that she'd locked her in. Nope. The door opened. Strange.

Harold stood at the top of the stairs whispering something to Anna before they both headed down. They were odd but they appeared to be kind. Kate went over to the bed and flopped onto it. She sunk and closed her eyes. She lay there for a few minutes and then got up and started poking around. The closet was bare, so she got on her hands and knees and looked under the bed. Nothing there either. She strolled over to the window and gazed down. Outside she could see Harold talking with a younger man. He towered over Harold. She couldn't hear what they were saying but they both looked pleased.

Kate backed away from the window when Harold looked up. Had he seen her? Stop it, Kate, you're acting paranoid now. You're nearly as bad as Frank.

Frank. She thought about him and Ella. After all she had been through, she couldn't wait to see their faces, give Ella a hug and get a decent night's sleep. Sleep had been sporadic so far. A few hours here, a few there.

Needing the washroom, she exited the room and padded down the hallway. She closed the door behind her and relived herself. She looked in the mirror and instinctively turned the tap on. It let out a groan but nothing came out except a trickle of dark water then it stopped. Why would you think there would be water? Idiot, she thought.

Her eyes looked at the shower curtain in the mirror, for a second she thought she saw a shadow behind it. Her pulse began beating hard. She turned and went over to it and pulled it back. Nothing there.

Shaking her head she exited the bathroom and passed by the bedroom Jake was in. She reached for the knob and gave it a twist but it was locked. Pressing herself up against it, she called out to him in a whisper. "Jake. You there?"

There was no answer. Why had they locked him in? Right then she heard the front door open and someone started coming up the stairs.

Chapter 20

Chester drenched the dead bodies in gasoline. He shook out a healthy dose of the flammable liquid. The boat wouldn't go up in flames as it was made out aluminum. Before this was done, Roy and him had dragged the three bodies into the boat and made sure they were positioned in a heap at the far end, away from the motor.

"Why didn't you put Donald in there?" Beatrix asked.

Chester tapped the side of his head. "I want them to think that he's still alive. Give them a reason to come over."

"I don't get it. Why don't we just go over?"

"That's what stupid people do. That's why your husband and his cousins died, isn't that right, Misty?"

She stood with her arms folded, looking pissed off. He could tell that she wanted to be in control. That she was used to throwing her weight around, but he was the one calling the shots now.

"First rule of hunting. To catch your prey, you have to outsmart it. Stay hidden, out of sight. Your scent has to be undetectable. You let it come to you. You bait it out of its comfort zone and once it's in the clearing. Bam! It's all over. As it stands we have the advantage. They are down ten people, eight if you don't consider the kids of any use. And just look at how easy it was."

"You killed four, we killed five, remember that," Misty said.

"Oh what, is this a game? Do you honestly need validation? Shut the hell up."

She scowled at him but he continued soaking the men in as much gasoline as possible. He wanted to make sure this shit could be seen from far away, as there was the chance it was going to veer off course.

"Okay, start up that engine, Roy. Let's get this baby back to its momma."

Roy hunched over and yanked on the cord. The engine roared to life. He then adjusted a lever close to the motor to keep the tiller handle stiff. He then opened up the throttle. As it began to move, he jumped in and tied off the throttle using some rope to hold it in place. He steered it out in the direction of the island, then tossed a lit flame on the bodies before diving over the side and swimming back to the dock.

Chester watched as the whole thing went up in a blaze of glory and the boat eased through the water towards Grindstone. Roy reached the dock and Bobby helped pull him up. Soaked and pissed off that he had to be the one to do it, he trudged past Chester without saying a word.

"There we go. Let's hope it reaches its destination."

"And if it doesn't?"

"They'll see it. Don't worry."

With that said, Chester turned and walked back down the dock, heading for the house. His work was done, at least for now. Now it was a waiting game. Frank Talbot wouldn't sit by idly. That wasn't the kind of man he was.

He cast a glance over his shoulder at the roaring fire in motion. "Are you ready, Frank?" he muttered under his breath. He snorted and pulled out a packet of cigarettes.

* * *

Frank had been nursing a bruised face and cut lip when Gabriel burst into the house calling for him. He was in the bathroom sitting on the edge of the tub while Ella tended to the swelling.

"Why would you just let him do that?"

"Because he needed to unleash his frustration. The way things were going I wouldn't have been surprised if he left the island."

He flinched as she touched the cut.

"I barely touched it."

"Well, it hurts."

The sound of Gabriel's boots and his yelling got his attention. He turned his head just as he came through the doorway.

"You need to come see this now."

"What is it?"

"Now."

He sighed and tossed the cloth down and followed

him out. "This better not be another couple wanting to leave the island. I've had enough of trying to mediate between those that want to stay and those that want to go. Frank hopped on to the back of the ATV and Gabriel gunned it across the green, nearly sending him flying off the back.

"Slow up, you're liable to get us both killed."

They'd already had one of the younger kids have an accident on one. Just because they had four wheels and it was low to the earth didn't mean that it couldn't flip. All it took was for a wheel to strike a tree root, or have them lose their grip and it was lights out.

"What are we doing here, Gabriel?"

"You'll see."

They exploded over a rise and caught a bit of air. Frank bounced when he hit the seat and they came to a halt ten feet away from the water's edge. Sal, Zach and Tyrell were already there looking out at the boat that was ablaze.

"That's Donald's boat," Zach yelled as Frank hurried

down to the water. They watched as it got closer. All of them backed up as it crashed against the rocks. Frank jumped on to one of the large boulders and stepped over to another until he could get a clear shot of what was alight. When he saw skin bubbling he diverted his gaze.

"Idiots!" Tyrell said.

"Is it all of them, Frank?" Sal asked. It was hard to see as the blaze had already turned what was in there into a charred mess. Putting up a hand he tried to get close and see but it was too hot. Instead, he came down to the edge and waded out into the water. Once he was close enough he began tossing water into the boat using a cupped hand. That's when Zach appeared. He came splashing through the water holding a bucket. Three, four, maybe five scoops and the fire was out. Nothing but the stench of burned flesh and smoke filled the air. They tugged the boat onto the land and tipped it over. The fragments of the dead scattered, some parts quickly being blown away like chaff in the wind. It was just a pile of black mess.

They all stood there gazing down, trying to make sense

of it. Tyrell kicked at one body, causing it to roll over. Warren. His entire back and legs were burned beyond comprehension but he hadn't died that way. It was the bullet holes that riddled his body that made it clear how they had died. Beneath him was Fergus. He was the only one whose body hadn't been as burned as the others. Beside him was Harry.

"Only three? Where's Douglas?"

Frank looked out over the water, wondering if he was still alive. And yet he assumed he couldn't be. Why would they keep him alive?

"Frank." Zach reached across the boat and yanked free a scrap of paper that was stuck between the engine and the boat. He opened it up to read.

You want to see Donald alive? You want to live? It's simple, just send over Frank Talbot.

As Zach muttered the words the rest of them looked at him.

"Did they sign off?"

"No. Just that."

Right then, Ella came over the rise and rushed down to the water's edge. "Holy shit" She backed up and put her top over the lower part of her face. Frank trudged out of the water. His clothes felt like a heavy weight wrapped around his waist.

"They're picking us off, one by one."

"No. That was just done to lure me out. It's me they want, no one else."

Frank didn't say anything.

"Where you going, Frank?" Sal asked.

"To get a get a shovel and bury the dead."

It was happening all over again. He had hoped they would be safe on Grindstone. Free from the horrors they had witnessed, but Ella was right — safety was an illusion. It didn't matter where they were, others would come and eventually try to take what they had. Though now it was human life.

* * *

Kate stood behind the door waiting for them to enter her bedroom. The footsteps were heavy. It wasn't Anna or Harold. It was the heavyset man she'd seen outside. She closed her door and wished there had been a lock on the other side. She heard his feet come up to her door and stop. The knob on the door turned and she breathed in deeply, preparing for the worst. Then, as if he had changed his mind, the man walked away. The sound of a lock. A door swinging on rusted hinges. Kate hurried over to the door and peeked out. There was movement; a groan, and then he reappeared; however this time he had Jake swung over his shoulder. What the hell? She gasped and then the man stopped in mid-step. His head turned, and she stepped back from the gap in the door. Shit! The rifle! Her eyes drifted around the room. Then she realized she'd left it in the kitchen. Damn it. When she heard the guy head downstairs, she moved back to the door and eased herself out. Moving quickly, she made it over to the staircase and peered down. She took one step and then Anna came into view. Kate's heart nearly stopped.

Fortunately, Anna walked past the stairs without even looking. Pressing her back against the wall, she descended slowly. She could still hear the man's boots, then a back door opening. Where were they taking him?

Not wanting to lose him, Kate rushed around the staircase, down through the hallway and past the basement door, which was open. The light was on. For a second, she contemplated going down to see if he had gone down there. Perhaps he didn't go out the back door, she thought. Maybe that was Anna. It was a toss up. Head down, or go out? First things first, she darted into the kitchen and saw her gun leaning against the wall. She grabbed it up. Outside, a cold wind was blowing, it was pitch dark and she couldn't see a damn thing. If he'd taken Jake out, where the hell were they?

Unsure of what direction to head in, and not wanting to waste any time, she decided to rule out the basement before going outside. Moving quickly, she navigated her way down the rickety wooden steps that shifted a little. There was no way she could have hidden the sound of her feet as the steps themselves were too old. They creaked every time she placed her foot down.

She could hear voices. The basement was unfinished. Nothing but stone floor and metal support beams. As she rounded the corner that led into a large room, she saw two tables with bodies lying on them. They were dressed in hospital garbs and moving ever so slightly. There was an EKG machine beating out a steady rhythm and IV drips set up.

Candles were dotted all over the room, casting ominous shadows that danced as she got closer. Kate hadn't made it within five feet of the bodies when one of them groaned and moved its hand. That's when she realized what she was looking at. They were two young children. A boy and a girl, no older than nine and twelve. Both were infected. She'd seen the symptoms enough to recognize it immediately. *Oh my god*. She backed up, heading towards the stairs and was about to rush up when the door opened and Harold and Anna were standing at the top. They stared at her for a second and then she raised the gun.

"Don't come any closer. What the hell is going on?"

Slowly, Harold made his way down. Kate moved back, keeping the rifle aimed at him.

"They are our grandchildren," he said, looking upon them despondently. "They were perfectly well yesterday until they contracted the infection."

"And the hospital equipment?"

"Taken from the hospital. It's been abandoned. We thought we could put it to use. Anna here has always worked in herbal medicine. She thinks that we might be able to cure them."

"I'm giving them a mixture of plant extracts," Anna added.

"It won't work. There is no cure."

"No. We don't believe that."

"You can believe whatever the hell you want. I don't give a shit. Now where is Jake?"

"Upstairs, dear," the woman said.

"Bullshit. I saw a man take him out."

"Oh, you mean Douglas. Our son. These are his kids."

"Where is he?" Kate said, shoving the rifle near them.

"Now why would you do that? After all we have done for you? We gave you food and a warm bed."

"You drugged him. You were going to drug me. Why?" She thought about the fish that she didn't eat.

"You're going to help us."

"What?" She shook her head. "Where is Jake?"

"Don't worry about Jake, he's not needed."

She couldn't believe what she was hearing. Were these people out of their fucking minds? "Listen up lady, you have until the count of three, or I'm going to blow your fucking brains out. Where is he?"

Mr. Rogers's lookalike stepped forward, trying to calm the situation. "Now Kate, calm down. All we want is for you to take a look at them."

It suddenly dawned on her. "Have you been anywhere near these children?"

"Well, of course we have."

Were they infected now? She backed up even more

fearful for her life. How could she have been so naïve?

"Don't come any closer," Kate said, hugging the wall with her back and working her way around the room until she reached the stairs. Though both Jake and her still had their masks on, Anna had tended to her leg. She had touched her bloodied leg with that cloth. Her mind swirled as the possibility of being infected hit her like a Mack train. She darted up the stairs and rushed outside through the kitchen and began screaming Jake's name.

"Jake! Jake!"

From behind her she could hear the sound of Harold and Anna, but she didn't stick around to find out what they were saying. She hurried out of the house and down the concrete steps, and that's when she saw the large, hulking man. He came out from one of the motel rooms, covered in blood. Raising her gun, she backed up.

"Get on the floor, now."

The bearded, heavy-set man kept walking towards her. She placed her finger on the trigger and readied herself to fire. From behind she heard the sound of Anna telling her not to shoot.

But it was too late.

She squeezed the trigger.

Nothing happened. It clicked. Then clicked again.

She turned and saw Harold remove a hand from his pocket and drop several bullets to the ground. Before she could respond, she felt a sharp thud against the back of her skull, and she fell to the ground. Her eyes rolled back in her head as words attempted to escape her lips. She rolled to one side trying to catch a breath.

The last image was of seeing the man drive the butt of her own gun down into her forehead, then everything went black.

Chapter 21

When Jake roused from his slumber, he squinted and raised a hand to block the glare of sunlight seeping through a window. What the hell? He couldn't move his arms or legs. As the world around him came back into view, he noticed that he was inside a motel room. There was a small TV in the corner, set on top of a chesterfield, and the curtains were drawn but the bathroom door was open. Again he tried to get up but it was impossible. Wire and rope cut into his wrists. His head was throbbing and he felt like he wanted to throw up. As he glanced down at his body, he noticed that he still had on his biohazard gear but it was torn, and he had several gashes on his leg.

What the hell happened? He had no recollection of how he had gotten there or who brought him in. His heart started beating faster. Then, slowly, memories of arriving in Dryden came back to him. They had eaten. That was the last thing he remembered — leaning back in a chair and closing his eyes.

Kate? He looked to his left and right. There was no one else in the room. It was early morning; the sun was just coming up.

Damn it! He berated himself for trusting them. He should have listened to Kate. No wonder they were so inviting. But that still didn't answer the question. Why? Why would they do this? It wasn't like they were carrying any supplies beside their weapons. It didn't make sense.

Survival instincts kicked in and he went through the full gamut of emotions. Jake struggled again to get loose but the restraints wouldn't budge. That was followed by an outburst of anger, then pleading and then acceptance. The only way he was getting out was if those assholes returned or if Kate... he sighed.

* * *

Two hours later, Kate was slapped back into consciousness with frigid water. Her eyes bulged and she attempted to sit upright as water dripped off her face. A voice echoed from inside the basement. She found herself chained to a pipe in a corner of the basement like a dog. Hell, she wouldn't have even treated a dog like that. They had given her a pillow to lie her head on, but beyond that she was just lying on the hard, unfinished ground.

"Finally, I thought you was going to sleep the day away. You have a lot to do."

"Why are you doing this?"

Anna turned with a look of confusion on her face.

"Isn't it obvious? You are going to cure our grandchildren."

"What?"

"Don't act surprised. In fact, consider yourself fortunate. Douglas was going to kill you. If I hadn't intervened, you would be under the earth by now."

"Why?"

Anna couldn't seem to make head or tails of what she was getting at. "Why what?"

"Why would he want to kill us?"

Anna moved closer to her and Kate shuffled back. "My daughter's name was Maria. She was a good girl.

Wouldn't harm a fly. When the pandemic began to spread, we all gathered here at the motel. It belonged to Maria and Douglas. Not long after. Two weeks in. Several men showed up here while we were out gathering medical supplies. They were infected, angry, and looking for a way to lash back at the world." She paused for a second as if trying to find the words to continue. "They tortured and murdered Maria. Now you have to understand. She would have offered them a bed for the night, warm clothes, and a hot meal. It was just in her nature to assist others. Maria was a God-fearing woman and yet for all her kindness, she was shown none."

"I'm sorry."

Anna shook her head. "No you're not. You don't know us."

"No, I don't. But it doesn't matter if I know you or not. We all are in this together." Kate glanced over at the children. "I understand what it feels like to lose someone you love to this virus. I understand that you want to find a cure but I'm telling you the truth. There isn't one. We spent every waking moment performing tests and researching new ways to attack the virus but failed. So if you expect me to cure them, you are going to be disappointed. They are going to die."

"If they die. So do you," Anna said, getting up and walking over to a shelf. She pulled a large white bucket and tossed it towards Kate.

"Use that to relieve yourself this morning. Once we have had breakfast, you'll begin."

Frustrated and angered by the way she was being treated, Kate slapped the bucket away.

"For God's sake. There is nothing here that you can give those children that will help them, Anna."

"Don't you dare take the Lord's name in vain."

Kate chuckled. "The Lord left the building a long time ago."

Anna screwed her face up, and balled her fist. This woman was beyond mentally unstable; she was full on schizo. "The Lord sent you. He has plans."

"Like what? Sitting around singing Kumbaya? Wake

up, Anna!"

"Oh, I'm wide awake. I know now what the Lord wants. Just as He shed His blood for us, you will shed your blood for them."

Kate frowned, trying to make sense of this madness. "What?"

"We are going to do a transfusion. Your healthy blood will be transferred into them."

Kate scoffed. "Are you out of your mind?"

She folded her hands. "Oh, I'm very clear." She smiled and started heading for the stairs. "I must get you and Jake prepped."

"Jake? Is he still alive?"

"Well of course, we're not savages."

Did she really hear that? Kate held up her chain in order to remind her.

"Precautions. It's for our safety."

Anna had climbed two steps and was muttering something when Kate shouted, "A transfusion won't work."

"It's used all the time for severe infections and liver disease."

"Dear God, woman, have you not been hearing a word of what I have said? This virus has no cure. Don't you think the CDC would have tried every approach?"

"The CDC creates viruses. I wouldn't be surprised if they released this to reduce population."

"Now you really are out of your mind."

Anna stepped back down and rushed over to Kate. She stabbed her finger in front of her face. "Science can only go so far. But the Lord, He will prove you wrong."

"You don't even know what blood type I am."

"It doesn't matter what type you are. The Lord has sent you."

With that said, she walked away holding a cross around her neck and mumbling under her breath some prayer. Kate rocked her head back against the hewn wall and sighed. Once Anna had disappeared, her eyes darted around the room for anything that might be within reach. The chain was connected to a set of handcuffs that was attached around a pipe. If she could find some metal that was thin or flat she could work her way out of the cuffs.

* * *

The door opened to the motel room and Jake glanced over to see Anna and a younger man.

"Hey, you want to get me out of this?"

"Settle down," Anna said.

"I'll settle the fuck down when you crazy bastards tell me why you are doing this."

"Full of questions, just like Kate. Well, all your questions will be answered soon enough. Douglas, go ahead and untie him and bring him up to the house, then go find your father and tell him to meet us in the basement. The Lord is going to raise up our little ones the way He did Lazarus."

Jake blinked hard. "Are you kidding me?"

Anna didn't reply. She exited the room and her large, hulking son headed over to the bed and started loosening his binds. He had a bald head and was dressed in dirty jeans, brown boots and a red and black plaid shirt. Once he'd loosened his binds, he kept a firm grip on the back of Jake's collar as he hauled him up and forced him towards the door. Jake knew that he only had minutes to figure out how to get out of this situation. It was now or never. As they stepped out into the bright morning light he lifted a hand to his face to block the glare.

"Move it."

Douglas shoved him forward but kept a tight grip. As he stumbled, he looked back under his arm, then reared his leg up and drove it hard into the Douglas right knee. He heard the crack, then the scream as Douglas fell to the gravel ground, gripping his knee in agony. Jake didn't wait for him to recover. He turned and launched his foot at his face multiple times, then stomped on his face four more times until he was unconscious. He raced towards the house, only casting a glance back at the bloody mess one more time before he hopped up the stairs, taking two at a time.

There was no way of knowing if they heard the scream but it was loud and he wasn't going to lose the window of opportunity. He burst through the front door. His eyes scanned the rooms. Where was the rifle? There was no time; he launched himself upstairs going room to room looking for Kate. Then he remembered what she'd said about meeting her in the basement. Jake raced downstairs and entered the kitchen. He scooped up a large knife out of the holder and was just about to head towards the basement when he caught out the side of his eye a mass moving in on him. It was fast and before he could react, he was slammed into the wall. The knife dropped to the ground and he looked up to see Douglas. No fucking way. He'd knocked him out. His face was barely recognizable. Blood dripped from every inch of his skin. His eye sockets were swollen, cut and suffocating his eyes. How could he even see?

He let out a large yell as he raised his foot up and drove it into Jake's chest. The air went out of him and he scrambled to escape. Douglas flipped over the table in the middle of the kitchen with one hand. It smashed against the counter and he grabbed a hold of Jake and lifted him with both hands, then swung him around like a rag doll. He tossed him out of the kitchen and down the hallway like a bowling ball. Jake slid across the hardwood floor and slammed into a small table with such force it broke apart. Several sets of keys, sunglasses and letters landed on the ground beside him. He groaned and his breathing was labored. A trickle of blood dripped from his head to the floor.

Douglas trudged down the long hallway, ready to finish him off. Out the corner of Jake's eye, in amongst the letters he saw a glimmer of silver. He reached for it as Douglas grabbed a hold of him. Clasped between his fingers was a letter opener. Just as Douglas was about to inflict even more pain on him, he jammed the sharp end of the letter opener up into his rib cage. Douglas roared in agony, still holding Jake by the back of his shirt. Jake twisted the steel blade.

Douglas staggered back. A hand reached for the letter opener and slowly extracted it from his gut. Jake rushed by him, heading for the knife in the kitchen. He was done fucking with this guy. As soon as he scooped it up he charged Douglas and drove the blade into him, sending him back to the floor. He pulled it out and continued to stab him multiple times until he stopped breathing.

Hunched over him, he exhaled hard, then rose up, yanking the blade free. Covered in blood, he approached the steps that led down to the basement. Out of breath, dizzy and nauseated from whatever they had given him, he made his way down the basement steps, keeping the knife out in front of him. As he turned the corner, his eyes fell upon Kate. She was strapped to a table and Anna was holding a knife to her throat.

"It's over. Step away from her."

She shook her head. "No, put it down or I will slice her from ear to ear."

This bitch was one crazy grandmother. He noticed that she had Kate hooked up to a machine, and she looked as if she was about to be hooked up to a child on the next table.

"I'm warning you, put it down," Anna yelled.

Fearing for her life, he held a hand out and tried to keep her calm. Slowly he lowered the knife.

"Kick it over here."

He grit his teeth and then gave it a kick. It slid across the concrete and disappeared under the table.

"Now get over there and attach one of your hands in that handcuff."

"Look, you don't need to do this. We'll go."

"Go? Why would you go? The Lord has sent you."

"The Lord? Lady, you are out of your fucking mind." He eyed the children. They were already close to death. One of them had blood coming out of his nostrils, the other was groaning and holding his stomach.

Anna held the knife hard against Kate's throat, causing her to gasp.

"Okay, okay, just don't hurt her."

Jake made his way over to the chain and took a seat.

"Put it on your wrist."

He sneered at her and slapped the cuff on. As the teeth caught hold he slumped down and she smiled. "There, now let's continue."

What Anna didn't see was that he had only clicked once. He left it wide enough that he could slip his hand back out. Sitting there on the ground, he kept his eyes on her, waiting for the right moment. She walked away from Kate and started to set up a tube that would go from Kate's arm to the child's. Slowly but surely he began working the cuff back and forth. It was painful but he'd done it numerous times in his security job. It was shown to them in the event they were ever handcuffed. There were several ways to get out. One way was to use a universal key, another was to insert a slim piece of metal, and the other was to work the hand out using spit. Rarely was the last way used because it relied on the cuffs not being fully engaged. If all the teeth were through, no one could get out; that's why he only put one piece through. He spat salvia down on to the hand and used it as lubricant to work his hand free.

Once it came loose, he waited for his moment to strike.

Chapter 22

The next morning, Frank was up long before the others were. He'd wrestled with his decision for the better part of the night. After they had buried the bodies, they held an emergency meeting in the home. Most of the remaining survivors gathered together, squeezed into the dining area, some of them spilling over into the kitchen. The conversation was heated at times. Fear dominated the topic of what needed to be done. Naturally people were scared. Scared to die. Scared to lose others. Scared to repeat what had occurred with Butch.

There was a total of twelve people in attendance. Some chose to not even show up.

"I say we go over," Jameson muttered. "We have more than enough people."

"Are you crazy? Four of our best went over and look what happened," Tom said.

Frank was in the corner. He said nothing, just

observed and listened. His eyes drifted over the Bolmer family, and then Mitch and Karla.

"Best?" Tyrell chuckled. "I wouldn't exactly call them our best. They returned looking like deep fried chicken."

"Tyrell," Gabriel snapped.

"Oh, whatever."

"Look, we have enough people to at least find out who's behind this," Zach said.

"Seems pretty obvious, we let Butch's brother and wife go. They are the only ones who would have a reason to kill," Tom muttered.

"Look, no one is going over there," Sal added. "No, we stay together this time. We have everything we need here. We don't need to venture out for at least another month or two. I say, we hole up here at the main house and we take turns patrolling the area. If we stay centralized, they can't pick us off."

"Excuse me if I find that hard to believe," Tyrell said. Frank rolled his eyes. The kid had no off switch. He had no idea of when not to speak.

"Frank, what do you think?"

He was leaning against a wall, lost in deep thought.

"They want me, none of you."

Sal scoffed. "You actually believe them?"

"If they wanted all of us, they would have attacked by now. Those deaths were just a message to me. Payback. Like poking a stick in a hornet's nest. They want me."

"So you are just going to waltz over there and hand yourself in?"

"Maybe."

Sal shook his head. "And what's that going to prove?"

"Nothing."

"Well then, that's not an option."

The conversation continued like that long into the night. Families ignored what Sal had to say about sticking together under one roof. By the time everyone retired for the evening, they were pissed off and nervous. And so they should. Up until that point, none of them knew who was behind it, how many people they were dealing with or when they might strike again.

So, at the crack of dawn, after much thought, Frank rose from his bed, shaved, washed his body and slipped into a clean set of clothes. He entered the room where Ella was sleeping and stood beside her for a moment. She made a groaning noise and rolled over. Even though she was a grown woman, he still saw his little girl. He would do anything to protect her, even if that meant handing himself in to avoid further bloodshed. He leaned in and landed a peck on her forehead, then left a note beside her pillow. It had taken him the better part of two hours to write it. It was one of several letters that he wrote that night.

After exiting her room, he placed one beside Gabriel's bed. He was snoring up a storm. Off to the right of him was Tyrell. He was scratching his balls and talking in his sleep. Even in his sleep he didn't know how to shut that trap of his. Frank smiled and walked back out. The last letter he delivered was to Sal. He slipped it under the door and then exited the home.

In the early hours of the morning, a heavy mist hung

over the river, a warm glowing sun was just coming up as he headed down to the dock with a bag over his shoulder. He stood at the foot of the shore and looked out across the river to his island. The place had been a haven for him for many years. Though the home was gone, the island itself held many fond memories. The older he got, the more sentimental he became about his family and past. He closed his eyes and breathed in the crisp air. For a few seconds his mind reverted back to being a kid. Back then there was no pandemic, no responsibilities and no hate. His life felt complete. He embraced endless summers, movie-filled weekends and a heart full of dreams. So much had changed.

He heard a branch snap behind him.

"Shouldn't you still be asleep?" Frank asked without even looking around.

"What are you doing, Frank?"

"I thought my letter explained it all."

Frank turned to find Sal gripping a letter. He made his way down to him. The sound of water gently lapping up against the boat was silenced by a flock of birds that broke in the trees.

"Oh, it did. But that doesn't mean it's right. What about Ella?"

"Look after her."

"And the others?"

"I think they will understand."

"They won't understand, Frank. Hell, even I don't."

Frank breathed a heavy sigh. "My entire life I have made decisions based around my fear. Selfish decisions. Decisions that have led to the breakdown of my marriage, a strained relationship with Ella, and now the deaths of others. Everything I have done has been selfishly motivated."

"Oh come on, Frank. We've all made selfish decisions."

"Not ones that have led to the deaths of others."

"No. No. You don't get to play the martyr here. We are all responsible. I chose to go with you to Queens. I set the events in motion just as much as you did. Had I stayed with Gloria, perhaps things would have been different."

"Maybe they wouldn't. You were right, Sal. We still had a choice. We were at a crossroads. We could have just moved on but we stayed and fought back, and look where it got us? Gloria is dead, Baily is dead, Hayley, Landon's family, Meghan, Donald and the list just keeps on going. How many more people have to die?"

"No, Frank. You can't carry that."

"Can't I? I already do and the weight of it is crushing me."

"There's another way around this."

"Is there? Because I don't see it."

"You know as well as I do they aren't just going to want you. So what, your plan is to go over there and attack? What happens if you get killed? Do you honestly think they are going to walk away? Huh?"

They studied each other. For a long time, Sal had questioned him about his life and decisions in their Thursday sessions together. It was tough back then but was even harder now. At least when he was in a session he knew that at the top of the hour, Sal would leave and everything would go back to normal — but not this time.

Frank kicked a few loose stones into the water and cast a glance across the misty river.

"And anyway, where is your weapon?" Sal asked.

"I didn't intend to bring one."

Sal's brow knit together. He chuckled. "For a second, I thought you were joking. But you're serious. You're not going over there to kill, you're going over there to be killed?"

"This ends today."

"And if it doesn't?"

Frank flung his hands up in the air. "He who lives by the sword dies by the sword."

"Oh, don't give me that bullshit. You're not religious."

"No, I'm not, but it's a valid statement." Frank grinned.

"So is... he who hands himself in without a gun, gets shot in the head. Come on, Frank, let's go back to the house. I know last night was heated but today's a new day. We can talk about it."

"I'm done talking." Frank headed down the short dock and got into the boat.

"Then I'm going with you."

Frank spun around and pointed at him. "No. You still have Adrian. That kid needs you."

"And Ella doesn't?"

There was silence. He swallowed hard, feeling himself get choked up.

"She's not a child anymore."

He turned and continued on.

"Frank!"

"You need to trust me, Sal. I've got to do this. For once, trust me."

"I never doubted you. I just don't agree."

Frank started the outboard engine and water bubbled to life. He glanced at Sal one last time.

"Look after her, Sal."

* * *

Jake watched as Anna went back and forth making preparations for a blood transfusion. Multiple times he tried to talk her out of it, but it was no use. The woman was clearly not in the right frame of mind. How many other minds throughout the country had cracked under the pressure and the fear of being infected?

Convinced that Jake was bound securely, Anna turned her back to insert an IV line into one of Kate's veins. In those few seconds, Jake placed the cuff on the floor and rushed forward. Anna spun around still holding the knife and tried to plunge it into Jake's heart. He reared back his foot and kicked her square in the stomach. She stumbled over the medical equipment and then came at him again. Jake grabbed her wrist as she brought the knife down and then gave her a right hook to the face. She went down for the count. He glanced at her for a second. She wasn't moving.

He hurried over to Kate and untied her wrist restraints; he then looked back at Anna while Kate continued to untie her feet restraints.

After the shit he went through with Douglas, he wasn't taking any chances. He walked over to where the knife had dropped and was just about to scoop it up when he felt a sharp pang in his leg. He turned to find Anna had grabbed his original knife that had slipped under the bed and sliced the back of his leg. He collapsed on the ground, dropping the knife only to have her slash him again. She rose up and loomed over him like a dark shadow.

"May the Lord have mercy on your soul."

She raised the knife to plunge it into him when she let out a gasp. Her eyes widened and blood burst forth. She staggered forward. Coming into view behind her was Kate. She had driven the knife he'd dropped into the back of Anna's neck. It protruded out the front and blood gushed as she dropped.

Kate's hand was shaking. She looked down at Jake and he exhaled.

He lifted a hand and she helped him up. They looked over at the two children.

"What about them?"

"There's nothing that can be done."

The kids were barely moving now. The virus had taken hold and robbed their bodies of all that was good. Jake and Kate hobbled over to the stairs and made their way back to the landing. Kate looked at Douglas as they stepped over him, before they headed toward the front door.

No sooner had they opened it, when they heard Harold's voice behind them.

"You've taken everything."

Jake turned to see him holding a handgun at his side. His hand was trembling. Jake hobbled a bit and tried to begin to reason with him.

"Look, it didn't have to be this way. If you'd just let us go."

Harold looked down at his son despondently. No emotion. Just emptiness in his eyes. "God forgive me."

As he uttered those words, he brought the gun up to his temple and squeezed the trigger. There was a loud crack and his body slumped to the floor. Jake's heart was pounding in his chest.

It was hard to imagine that people could be full of so much anguish that they would go to any lengths, including harming others, in order to save the sick. But with no doctors or hospitals in operation, folks were left with taking matters into their own hands.

"Holy shit," Kate said, staring blankly at them. "Let's get out of here."

Jake nodded but didn't say a word.

Before they left they took what weapons they could find, a set of keys to a silver Volkswagen, a bag full of crackers, and left behind a cupboard full of sardines.

Chapter 23

The G3 1652 DK camo welded boat powered across the waves as a cold, westerly wind battered Frank. His mind was too preoccupied by what lay ahead, and the decision he'd made, to notice the thick black tarp moving. When he finally heard it shift, it startled him. He frowned and leaned over, pulling at the tarp.

"Eva, what are you doing here?"

She looked up at him, grinning. She was a holding a Walther P22, and beside her was a Heckler & Koch MP5. Frank throttled down and she got up.

"It's not the first time I've visited the mainland."

"What?"

"I've been over there several times. I thought you might need a hand."

"I'm taking you back right now."

"You're not going to stand a chance against them. I've seen them."

"What?"

He turned the boat then slowed it down.

"I went over with Donald and the others. They didn't know I was there."

"But you weren't in the boat that returned."

"I couldn't get back in but I saw what happened to them. Donald isn't over there. He's dead. The cop shot him."

"The cop?"

"One of them was wearing a cop uniform. He seemed to be the one in charge as he was barking orders at the others. And the lady, I'd seen her before too. I don't know her name, but she was one of the group that entered the Metro store on the Canadian side. Though she doesn't appear to be with the others. Just her and another woman."

"Describe to me what this cop looked like?"

"I dunno, six foot, maybe taller with dark hair."

"No, I mean the uniform."

As she began to describe the color, Frank's stomach

sunk. It was Chester. It had to be. He knew the guy was a lunatic, but the fact that he traveled all this way north meant he wasn't just going to walk away. Even if he killed Frank, he would come after the others.

This changed everything.

"How many were there?"

"Hard to say, maybe six or seven at the most if you include the two women."

Frank killed the engine and the boat just bobbed in the water shrouded by the morning mist.

"How did you get back?"

"I found a kayak."

This girl was more resourceful than some of the others on the island. And through it all she had never once complained. If only they had more people like her, Frank thought.

"Why didn't you tell us last night?"

"Because then I would have had to explain how I knew. And no offense, but I like my freedom."

"Freedom? Hiding in a boat. You could have got

yourself killed. How many others times have you visited the mainland since we brought you back?"

"A couple of times. And anyway, I can look after myself."

"Yeah, I can see that. Give me those guns."

He took them from her and placed them out of her reach.

"I know how to shoot."

"How?"

"My father taught me."

"You're ten."

"So? You must have taught Ella when she was that old."

"No. I kept my guns out of reach and out of sight."

Eva shrugged.

"Anyway, how the hell did you know I was leaving for the mainland?"

"I didn't. I was using the bathroom when I heard you walking down the hallway. What did you say in those letters?"

"It doesn't matter."

"I'm sure it will matter to Ella."

"I'm taking you back," Frank said, starting the engine.

"You know how my parents died?"

She hadn't ever mentioned how, only that they had.

"No," he said, annoyed that he was going to have to head back and then no doubt end up in a debate with Sal again about leaving. Then there was Ella. If she was awake now, there was no way in hell she was going to let him just waltz into the lion's den. Then again, finding out that it was Chester changed everything. Frank had initially thought it was Bret — nothing more than a brother lashing out over the death of Butch. He figured he could reason with him. It was risky and there was a chance he could have been shot, but at some point society had to lay aside their weapons and communicate with each other. Of course there would always be those that would say that was dumb and that after a pandemic the only thing people would understand was a bullet, but he had to believe that wasn't the case with everyone. Sure, Landon,

Hayley and the others had died, but he didn't know what kind of conversation they had before it happened. Had they tried to bargain with Landon? Were they in the same store at the same time as Hayley and Meghan? Or was it just a cold-blooded killing? An act of revenge for the death of Butch and his cousins?

Eva continued. "My mother died from the virus but my father was murdered. I saw it happen. There was a group that broke into our home, looking for supplies. My father told me to exit by way of the upstairs window and to head over to my uncle's store. I did as he said but not before sticking around to find out what happened to him. I heard him try to bargain with them. He was going to give them half of what he had but they wouldn't listen. They shot him in the kitchen. I was watching from outside."

"I'm sorry to hear that."

"I would do anything to have my father back. Ella needs you. Going over there to talk to them isn't going to get you anywhere. Donald tried to talk to them but that cop shot him and kicked him into the water like he was a piece of trash." She paused. "I can help you."

Frank shot her a sideways glance.

"I'm sure you can. For someone who's only ten, you've had to grow up fast."

"Eleven, not ten."

"Excuse me," Frank smirked.

"You don't want them to die, do you?" Eva asked. Water splashed up the sides of the boat, waves lapped against the front. "That's why you are going in alone."

He nodded but didn't clarify his reasons. It wasn't just a case of not wanting others to die, he didn't want to be held responsible for making another decision that would haunt him. The look on Sal's face after losing Gloria and Bailey was hard enough to bear.

As they got closer to Grindstone Island, Frank squinted. At the shore's edge, barely visible through the early morning mist, stood several figures. The closer they got the more he could tell who it was. Armed and preparing to enter boats were Sal, Gabriel, Zach, Ella,

Jameson, Tyrell, Tom Hannigan, Mark Bolmer, Mitch and Karla.

Frank shook his head and smiled as he brought the boat into the dock. Eva was the first to hop out, followed by Frank. Sal pointed at her and told her to get into the house like a father might. Ella stood with her arms crossed and her gaze narrowed.

"After this is over, me and you are going to have a talk," Ella said. She didn't say any more than that. She boarded a boat with Gabriel and Tyrell and the others followed suit. Sal approached Frank and a smile danced on his lips.

Before Frank could say anything, he spoke. "This is our decision, not yours. Whatever happens today is because we chose to go. No more guilt, you hear me? And I didn't coerce them. We know you risked your life to ensure our survival, now let us do the same for you."

Frank sighed and shifted his weight from one foot to the next. He gazed around at the others listening in. There was strength to them that he hadn't seen the previous night. Whether Sal had convinced them or simply told them that Frank was about to head in alone would remain unclear for now, but either way it was good to see that they were ready to fight.

"If you are going to do this. Don't do it for me. Do it for yourselves, do it for Landon and his family, Hayley, Meghan and the four men," Frank said.

"So what's the plan?" Tyrell asked.

"Don't get shot," Gabriel replied before starting his boat. Tyrell gave him a punch on the arm.

"Listen, there is no more than six, maybe seven of them, Eva said. They are holed up on Washington Island. Gabriel, take your boat to the west tip, and work your way in from that side, Mark and Tom, you are going to approach from the east. Sal and I will come from the north. Keep back, let us go in first. I don't want them spotting you all. The rest of you circle around to the south side and work your way in. We don't want them escaping via the causeway, so someone remain posted near the entrance." Frank stepped back into the boat, and Sal joined him. "Oh, one of them is Misty, and another is a cop. Don't hesitate to shoot, as they won't. There will be no discussion. I don't wish for more bloodshed, but what we do now, we do for our survival. This ends today."

Frank nodded slowly, inhaled deeply and got back into the boat. Outboard motors roared to life and water spluttered as they began easing out, heading for the mainland.

Chapter 24

Chester had posted Roy, Bobby and Sawyer at various places on the North side of Washington Island throughout the night. In the event that Talbot attacked in retaliation to the string of murders, he was going to be ready. Meanwhile, the others stayed in two of the homes located right in the center of the island.

There were only eighteen homes on the island from what they could tell. They had spent the night going through each one and gathering what supplies they could find. Chester couldn't believe that everyone had just simply upped and left, except for that poor sod who had offed himself with pills. That was a nasty sight. The place stunk to high heaven of rotting flesh.

They ended up sleeping in number twenty-four, a brown clapboard, one bedroom home with almost eight hundred square feet of living space and a pool in the backyard. Hell, Chester had even been tempted to take a dip as the owner had covered over the pool, and so the water below it was still as fresh as the day they had filled it.

Instead, he spent that evening getting acquainted with Misty's friend, Rachel. Unlike Misty, she was more than willing to put out and damn did she ease some of the tension.

As Chester came out that morning, leaving Rachel naked and entangled in bed sheets, he passed by Misty, who was coming out of the bathroom. She slung him a dirty look and he just waved her off. "You missed out."

"Screw you," she said as she walked away. He cast a glance back and licked his lip. Before the week was over he would break down that hard exterior of hers and have her begging for it. Chester strolled into the bathroom looking all pleased with himself. He got within two feet of the toilet and winced. The smell was atrocious. Then he heard Misty let out a laugh.

"I left you a gift."

Chester peered over and saw a large shit in the toilet.

She hadn't just taken a shit, but smeared it all around the seat.

"That is fucking nasty."

"Perhaps that will make you think twice," she said before disappearing into a room. He backed away from the tube steak clogging up the toilet and chose to take a piss in the sink instead. He was in mid-stream when Roy burst into the house yelling his name. Oh for fuck sake, what now, he thought.

"Can a guy not take a piss in peace?"

"Chester!"

"What is it?" he yelled as he finished up.

"We got company."

His eyes flared and he double-timed it out, shot into the bedroom and nearly fell over while trying to get dressed.

"Get up."

Rachel groaned and he spanked her on her bare ass. "Wake up, I need everyone ready."

He was still doing up his belt buckle as he stumbled

down the stairs to find Roy pacing up and down with his rifle in hand.

"Who is it?"

"Frank Talbot and his pal."

"Sal?"

He nodded.

"Perfect. Where are they?"

"North side."

"Bobby and Sawyer?"

"Still over there."

"Get on the radio and tell them not to shoot them. They are to bring them in alive. I want to see him before he dies."

Misty came down the stairs with a pump action shotgun.

"You're staying here," Chester said.

"The fuck I am. He's mine."

Chester grabbed hold of the barrel of her gun and pointed at her. "I didn't come all this way to have you fuck this up."

"And my husband didn't die just so you can take Talbot's last breath. You owe me."

"Owe you? I owe you shit."

"Without me you wouldn't have even known he was on Grindstone Island."

Chester cocked his head to one side. She had a point. There were a few seconds where he contemplated how to deal with it. He wanted to be the one to see the light leave Talbot's eyes. He didn't want it to be over quickly. No, he wanted to toy with him, break him down, make him grovel, then make him think he was going to release him and then, and only then, just when he thought they were even, he would snuff his light out. But, there was the fact that letting Misty do it might allow him a way to wiggle his way into her good books. He could see himself taking her back to the cabin. With the whole world gone to shits, he was going to need someone to wet his dick.

"Alright, but we do it my way. He's not to die immediately, understood? When I'm done with him, then he's all yours."

She narrowed her eyes and gnawed on the side of her lip. "Agreed."

With that said, they rushed out the main door while Roy led the way.

* * *

"Do you honestly think he's going to believe us?" Sal asked as they brought the boat in and hopped out.

"He'll buy it."

Sal shook his head not convinced as he tied off the boat. While he was doing that, Frank was eying the other homes nearby. They were watching. That he was sure of. No one came this far north to be caught with their pants down.

"And if he shoots us?"

"Oh trust me, he won't. You don't come this far to fire a bullet and walk away. There's a reason why he left us alive that day he jumped us. Just as there was a reason he let us leave Lowville. He's no Butch Guthrie."

"No, maybe not, but if Misty is with him, she is."

"Sure but Chester is an egomaniac. He's not going to

let some skirt call the shots. You only had to listen to him drone on about the women he had banged to understand how he sees them. They're nothing to him except a means to get off."

"What about the weapons?"

"Leave them."

"Leave them?"

"If we want him to buy this, we can't give him any reason to think we are trying to screw him over. With no weapons, he'll expect us to try and work it out without violence."

"Misty won't."

"Don't worry about her."

"You know, Frank, you have pulled me into some crazy shit since this has kicked off, but this by far tops it."

"Remember what you said."

"You are going to bring that up every chance you get, aren't you?"

"Of course," Frank grinned as they made their way down the rickety old dock towards a sandy path that snaked its way around multiple boulders.

No sooner had they walked between two homes when two men came into view. Frank remembered them both from that night in the woods. Both were armed. They didn't say a word. They simply motioned with their guns where they were to go.

Once they reached them, they patted them down. A bead of sweat dripped down Frank's face. Their hands went up between their legs, around the outside, under his arms and down the outside.

"Okay, you're good."

A sigh of relief flooded his being. It had worked.

Frank placed his hands behind his head and nudged Sal to do the same. Reluctantly Sal interlocked his fingers behind his head and they walked forward in front of the two men around a winding road until they could see Chester in the distance. He stood with his weight to one side and a smug grin on his face. An MP-5 hung loosely in his right hand. Frank's eyes drifted over the rest of them. Misty sneered as they got closer.

Chester slung the MP-5 over his shoulder and began clapping slowly.

"Frank Talbot and Sal Hudson. What a surprise to see you both again, and unarmed! Really? I would have thought you two had learned from your last experience, but then again you weren't exactly spilling over with intelligence the first time I met you both."

He looked around.

"So where are the others?"

"Just us. I thought we could talk. Man to man."

Chester scoffed and looked at his cousins. "Man to man? You thought we could talk? Oh, that is priceless. Cute even. Unfortunately Frank, my grace extends only so far. I would have thought after our discussion in Lowville I made that crystal clear. But you just couldn't do it, could you? You had to push it. Well, now you are going to pay."

Frank shook his head. "I was really hoping it wouldn't come to that."

"Well you were wrong. Misty, would you like to do

the honors?"

She smiled and turned over her rifle as if preparing to use the butt to give them a beating.

"By all means."

"Come on, Chester. We can talk this through. There is no need for more bloodshed."

He took a few steps back. "Sorry, it's out of my hands now."

Misty started making her way towards Frank. With his hand locked behind his head and Chester's men ahead of them, his fingers slipped down behind his neck and beneath his jacket. His hands clasped around the handles. He was just about to pull them when Tyrell opened his mouth.

"Hey, douche bags!"

Fuck! Frank thought, every damn time. That kid just didn't know when to keep his trap shut.

Frank smiled.

And yet, the beauty of it was his timing couldn't have been better. Misty and the others jerked their heads towards Tyrell who stood with Gabriel a short distance away on the west side.

"Hey, over here," another voice cried out. Again they turned to the east and saw Tom and Mark strolling up with their rifles aimed in their direction.

"And don't forget us." The others appeared from the south behind them.

Those distracted seconds were all he needed.

Prior to leaving that morning he had attached two Glock 22s into a makeshift holster that was secured to his upper back. He knew he'd be patted down, but like most pat downs, people rarely checked the top half of someone's back.

Frank pulled them out in one smooth motion and squeezed the triggers, unloading two rounds. One struck Bobby in the side of the face, obliterating his jaw, the other struck Sawyer in the temple, tearing through his skull. Frank elbowed Sal to seek cover as he pulled back, firing a third and fourth time. Gunfire erupted from both sides as Chester and those remaining returned fire.

Everyone scattered seeking cover but it was virtually impossible. The only areas that offered any protection from the bullets snapping furiously in the air were the houses, single trees and bushes.

The look of utter terror on Chester's face at the realization that he was surrounded only increased as another one of his men hit the dirt. Frank and Sal sought shelter behind a thick oak tree out the front of a home.

"Okay, what was that you said about no weapons?"

"I lied."

"Lied?"

"What? Did you really think I was going to go in there unarmed? You are out of your mind!" Frank said, smirking before unleashing another flurry of rounds. Sal was on his belly trying to keep his head down.

"Out of my mind? What the fuck? Hey! You think I could get one?"

"Oh right, yeah, here you go."

He tossed one to Sal, and he shook his head.

"After this, I swear I'm going to extend our one hour

session to two. You have some serious underlying issues."

Frank laughed.

The fighting intensified, three of Chester's men were dead, and all that remained were four and that included Chester. Chester had managed to sprint back into a house. Frank tore after him, zigzagging his way across the lush green yards while the others continued to push in against Misty and two other women.

When Frank made it to the back of the house, he pressed his body against the wall and listened. He could hear movement inside. Rustling and cursing, then the front door opened. Frank spun into the back of the house and in a crouched position he pressed on until he saw the front door. Thinking he was trying to make a break for it, he rushed towards it only to hear the crack of a gun from behind him. A burning sensation spread through his shoulder as he hit the ground. A slug had struck him in the right shoulder. He landed hard and his gun slipped across the floor. Coming into view just a few feet away was Chester.

"Like I said, you never struck me as someone who had much intelligence."

He leveled his gun to fire. "Bye, Frank."

A round erupted and Chester spun to the ground. Another one exploded and his body went limp. Groaning on the floor and trying to get up to see who had shot him, Sal came into view. He loomed over Chester's body and then fired another one into him.

"Maybe if you had been intelligent you would have looked behind you, asshole."

Frank clutched his bloodied shoulder and Sal came over and helped him up. Frank opened his mouth as if to speak but Sal raised a finger.

"Don't say a word." He gestured with his head. "Come on, let's go."

Frank stumbled outside, wincing in pain. Silence had once again returned to the small island and peaceful neighborhood. Dotted around in various places were the bodies of the dead. Ella stood over Misty, her gun still pointed at her. Misty was motionless. Frank went over and pried the gun from Ella's stiff hand.

"It's okay hon, it's over."

She wrapped an arm around his waist and they wandered over to the rest that were gathered together in the middle of the road. They were standing near Tom's lifeless body. A bullet had struck him in the chest. Mark was sporting a bullet wound to his leg. The rest appeared to be fine.

Though it was over, Frank couldn't help but wonder what may have happened if it had just been him that arrived. Perhaps it would have been him lying face down in the road. Though Tom had been reluctant to fire a gun in the past, he had finally come through when it mattered most. Mark said that he killed one of Chester's men just before he died. Had he not had the courage to squeeze off a round, Mark wouldn't have made it.

Frank looked over his shoulder at the dead as they carried Tom back to the boat.

There was no glory to be found that day. Neither would they celebrate.

For though they would live to see tomorrow, others wouldn't, and regardless of who was right or wrong in Frank's mind, that wasn't victory.

Epilogue

A deep orange sun, burned brightly in the sky that afternoon as Tom's body was laid to rest. His wife, distraught by the news, found comfort in knowing that he had risked his life in order to save another. She put on a brave face that day, as she crumbled soil in her hand over the mound of dirt. Many tears would follow in the coming weeks. They always did. Shock numbed people to the real pain. The kind of pain that would be experienced later, in times of quietness, when those that checked in on folks had left and all that remained was the echo of one's own thoughts.

Two days later, after everyone had retreated to his or her spots on the island, Frank sat out on the back porch sipping on iced tea and nursing a painful shoulder. It would become one of many days that he would spend resting. Sal had gotten back into the swing of psychoanalyzing him and had given him strict instructions not to lift a finger. He fancied himself as a doctor and had been reading up on medicine using Landon's old library.

Frank glanced out at his island and brought a hand up to his eyes to block the glare of the light reflecting off the waves. He'd stopped rebuilding the house that he had plans for, not because he didn't want his old home back, but simply for the fact that his home was now where the others were.

Ella appeared in the doorway before stepping out and joining him on the porch rocker. They sat there for a few minutes saying nothing. The smell of summer lingered in the air; pine trees, wild flowers and the river. As small waves lapped up against the boulders and the stress of the morning faded, Ella cleared her throat.

"I read the letter," she said.

His eyebrows rose, unsure of what she would say. He thought he had managed to duck that conversation. But she was just been biding her time, probably thinking about how to approach him. That's what he admired about Ella. Unlike him, she was prone to dwell on matters and give them careful thought before rushing. It was her strength and his weakness.

"First, you never failed me as a father."

"But your mother."

"It happens. If anything, this pandemic has taught me that some things are out of our control. We don't get to control the future, only how we choose to react."

He cocked his head to one side and picked at his pant leg. "But I could have tried harder."

"Perhaps," she paused, "but wisdom is in hindsight, right?"

"I guess."

"And this business of me not needing you. I might not be dependent on you, but I always want you in my life."

He glanced at her and squinted. "How did you grow up on me so fast, kid?"

"I didn't have much choice."

"Point taken."

She was about to continue when Sal came out.

"Please tell me you are not here to give me another earful," Frank joked. "I'm not due to see you until Thursday."

"Actually, I thought you might want to see this."

Frank's heart sunk at the thought of more trouble. He rose from his seat and scooped up his rifle.

"You won't need that," Sal said.

"No? Why, you got two Glocks strapped to your back?"

He laughed. "Funny man. Seriously, come on."

"Hold that thought Ella, I'll be right back."

"Actually, she's going to want to see this."

Her eyebrows shot up and she smiled. As they made their way outside, Sal continued yapping about how he was thinking of offering his services to the others on the island. He figured that he could probably do pretty well now since there were so many folks struggling to deal with their issues. When asked how he was going to accept payment, he commented that they could give him moonshine. Jameson had learned the recipe from Abner

Rooney and he was using it for trading. Everyone on the island was beginning to think differently. Trading would become the norm, no one person would govern over everyone and each person would look for new ways to contribute.

As they made their way down to the shore, Frank was expecting to find another boat full of dead bodies, instead what he found made him stop in his tracks.

Standing by a small paddleboat that had docked alongside the shore's edge was a small crowd. Gabriel, Tyrell, Zach and Jameson were all talking. In the midst of them were two people. One wearing a security uniform and the other... his eyes widened. Even after all the years that had passed he could recognize her from behind.

She turned her head at the sound of them approaching and smiled.

Frank stared at Kate as Ella raced on and entered her embrace. Her eyes remained fixed on him as she kissed Ella and held her tightly.

Sal leaned in and whispered. "This time, don't screw it

up."

Frank elbowed him in the rib and he let out a groan.

"That's going to cost you two bottles of moonshine," he muttered.

Slowly, Frank made his way down, his mind no longer distracted by the pain of his arm. Kate broke away from Ella and met him halfway. They stood there, a gap between them and stared at each other for a second.

He smiled. "Kate."

"Frank."

There was an awkward pause. "Oh, um, this is Jake," she thumbed over her shoulder. "He helped me get here."

Frank nodded. "Nice to meet you, Jake."

Jake extended his hand. Frank glanced at it for a second, then back at him.

"Oh, he doesn't—"

Before Kate could finish saying that he didn't shake hands, Frank smirked and stepped forward and shook it. Her brow knit together. The look of surprise on Kate's face made both Ella and him laugh. Without saying another word, Frank followed up by giving Kate a warm hug with his good arm.

"It's really good to see you," he said.

"But... I thought...?" she looked shocked. Her eyebrows shot up, then she smiled. "You've changed."

"More than you know," he muttered. "More than you know."

As he turned to lead them back towards the house, he winked at Sal. Sal returned a nod of approval.

* * *

THANK YOU FOR READING
Strain: (The Agora Virus Book 3)
Please take a moment to leave a review.

.

A Plea

Thank you for reading Strain. If you enjoyed the book, I would really appreciate it if you would consider leaving a review. Without reviews, an author's books are virtually invisible on the retail sites. It also lets me know what you liked. You can leave a review by visiting the book's page. I would greatly appreciate it. It only takes a couple of seconds.

Thank you — **Jack Hunt**

Newsletter

Thank you for buying Strain, published by Direct Response Publishing.

Click here to receive special offers, bonus content, and news about new Jack Hunt's books. Sign up for the newsletter. http://www.jackhuntbooks.com/signup/

About the Author

Jack Hunt is the author of horror, sci-fi and post-apocalyptic novels. He currently has three books out in the Camp Zero series, five books out in the Renegades series, three books in the Agora Virus series, one out in the Armada series, a time travel book called Killing Time and another called Mavericks: Hunters Moon. Jack lives on the East coast of North America.

Made in United States
Orlando, FL
13 February 2023